Beneath
the
Blue Bridge

VALE ROYAL WRITERS GROUP

ACKNOWLEDGEMENTS

Cover design by JT Lindroos
Cover photograph by Geoff Leigh

Special thanks to *The Blue Cap* in Sandiway for hosting our meetings and providing refreshments.

INTRODUCTION

Another anthology of short stories, prose and poetry from
Vale Royal Writers Group in Cheshire.

The second anthology *Under the Red Umbrella* can be found on
Amazon, or bought from the VRWG committee.
The first anthology *The Cheshire Collection* is now out of print.

Members come from all walks of life – some no longer live in
Cheshire but remain associated with the group, united by their
love of our county and of writing.

VRWG meets monthly in Sandiway. For more information,
check out **www.vrwg.co.uk** or find us on Facebook at
www.facebook.com/groups/ValeRoyalWritersGroup/

CONTENTS

Carolyn O'Connell

ISLAND

When they met she was in black —
her red lips a splash of hope —
and he caught her by the door:
she had stopped in the light,
named by the etched glass,

a kiss before he left for the boat.
It was one remembered by her
but was not spoken of until
she was forced to admit the truth.

Summer was the time we travelled
away from the city to new places
where sea scented the days, mingling
with fruits from her orchard.

We gulped thyme, garlic that grew
wild on the hills above the bay,
broke the glass water as a pair
of eagles frolicked over the island.

Her cups were stacked carefully,
brought out for tea when guests came
together with cake stacked
neatly on stands above white cloths,
so the ceremony would always be perfect.

The city clouds, the moist heat had thrust
me inside. I found a photo of them
taken in that lost light.

Published Reach Poetry 229, October 2017

Deborah K Mitchell

SON OF MINE

The kettle boiled just as the front door slammed, and heavy footsteps thundered across the tiles in the hall and up the stairs. The pace was quicker than usual. Something he wanted to catch on TV, maybe. Or an urgent need to update his Facebook status.

'Tea, Dan?' I shouted up the stairs. He liked a cup when he got home from college. It had become part of our late afternoon routine since he started at the Sixth Form.

Routine suited my Daniel. It soothed him. Always had.

I heard his bedroom door click shut.

'Dan,' I repeated. 'Kettle's just boiled.'

No answer.

Probably had his headphones on. He never hears a thing when he's wearing those. World War 3 could kick off, and our Dan would be in his little happy bubble, listening to music or playing on the Xbox, oblivious to everything around him.

I filled his mug with English Breakfast tea – his favourite – and emptied a couple of chocolate chip cookies onto a plate, before carrying the lot on a tray up the stairs. I tapped my toe against his bedroom door.

'Here you are love. Tea and biscuits. Can I come in?'

No reply.

I tapped again.

Again, nothing.

Rather than barge in and risk the embarrassment of catching him in a state of undress, or doing whatever private things teenage boys do behind closed doors, I edged my way in, waving a hand before opening the door fully. Usually by now, he'd have been alerted to my presence and taken his headphones off.

But he didn't have them on. He was sitting on the edge of

the bed, facing away from me, and he was shivering. Quite violently. So much so, that the glass of water on the bedside cabinet was rattling against the lamp.

'Daniel?'

I put the tea-tray down and went to him.

'Love, what's the matter?'

He stayed in the same position, so I could only see him from the side. He was hunched over, leaning forward on his knees, and his legs were moving up and down; something I'd seen him do when he was nervous or agitated. His hair fell forward, covering his face.

I moved over to the side of the bed to stand in front of him.

At first, I thought it was a pattern on his sweatshirt. But then realised that he didn't own a top that looked like that. The red was in huge blotches across the fabric, with more patches of red on his jeans.

He lifted his head. Blood was smeared across his cheeks and neck.

'Mum.'

He began to sob. Quietly at first, but then louder, more anguished, as if he was in agony.

I wrapped my arms around him and hugged his shaking body to me.

'What happened Daniel? What happened? Are you hurt?'

He shook his head, but no words came. I buried my nose in his thick hair, smelling shampoo and the metallic tang of blood. He continued to cry. To tremble. I held him closer still. The room began to darken as night closed in. Eventually, after what felt like hours, he was still, and silent.

I got up and closed the curtains, turned on the bedside lamp, sat back down on the bed next to him.

'Daniel. You've got to tell me what happened to you. Why are you covered in blood?'

My son. An 18-year-old man-child. Two days' stubble on his chin. His complexion, creamy smooth as strawberry milkshake. He stared at me with huge dark blue eyes, which right then spoke of pain.

He rubbed his nose and eyes on a sleeve, and pushed the hair away from his face. His voice was husky when he spoke.

'I didn't mean to do it,' he said. 'I just couldn't stand it anymore.'

'Dan, tell me about the blood.'

He twisted away from me, and ran his hand under a pillow, grabbing hold of something I could not see, until he turned back.

'Whose is it, sweetheart?' I could hear the tremor in my voice, and feel my heart thumping.

'His. I took it, and...'

'Hand it to me, love.'

Daniel shook his head and gripped the knife by its handle. The blade rested across his right wrist. I stroked his shoulder.

'We can talk about this, Daniel, but I want you to give me the knife so you don't hurt yourself.'

I reached out a trembling hand.

'Please, love.'

'No, no, no!' He grew more agitated and began to shake again. I watched the blade skim over the pale skin on his wrist, watched it brush against the blue of his vein. 'He made me do it. He made me. You've got to believe me.'

He leaned forward on his knees again and moaned, long and hard. Spittle fell in strings from his mouth. Tears formed tracks through the blood smears on his face. Our arms were touching, but he felt a million miles away.

His clock, always placed exactly four centimetres from the edge of the second shelf in his bookcase, ticked away the seconds that we sat, motionless and silent now, on the bed. The knife lay next to him; its blade speckled red.

Everything in Daniel's room had its place. But right then, he didn't. Dishevelled and dirty and smelling of sweat and blood, my son had become alien in his own environment.

I got up from the bed and sat on his wicker chair, opposite him.

He gazed, glassy-eyed at me.

'It was Byron. He sat behind me on the bus,' he said.

Byron Reynolds. The wayward little shit who had been a thorn in our side since he and Daniel were at primary school. A rootless boy with a father and mother who took more interest in their violent arguments and cheap cider, than their own child.

'He started to taunt me about my Asperger's. Said I was a loony. Poked me in the back and pulled my hair. No one took any notice.'

My hands instinctively balled into tight fists. My beautiful, soulful, clever boy exposed to an insensitive, cruel world which viewed him as an oddball, rather than someone to be cradled and nurtured.

'He got off at my stop and followed me, shouting horrible things and throwing stones. And then he grabbed me, just as we were passing the service alley at the back of the shops. He pulled this out of his pocket...'

Daniel picked up the knife, and handed it to me.

'He pushed me up against the bins and put the blade against my throat, and told me I was a gay psycho who deserved to die.'

The knife felt heavy and terrible in my hands, so I laid it carefully on the floor, never taking my eyes off my son.

'I struggled to get away, and the next thing the knife was in my hand and ...'

Daniel swallowed hard and bowed his head.

'... the next thing I knew, he was on the ground, with blood pouring out of his chest, and the knife was still in my hand. I killed him, mum.'

Bile rose from my gut and burned the back of my throat. I reached across to the bedside cabinet for the glass of water, and drank it all.

My Daniel had acted in self-defence. The police would be sympathetic, surely? They would see how it was all a tragic accident. Even if they charged him, a jury would never convict my son. How could they?

I had to dial 999. Explain what had happened. Volunteer to take him down to the station, so they could see him. See how vulnerable he is. Special. My special boy.

Daniel pulled his legs up under himself and curled up on the bed. Like a baby. Small and delicate. I wanted to wrap him up in a soft blanket and protect him from everything that was bad.

Bad, like a prison cell. Like endless days trapped behind high walls. Like being bullied by vicious screws and violated by angry inmates. How would my fragile child cope with a life inside? It would kill him. I knew it.

'Listen to me carefully Daniel,' I said. 'I'm going to take the tea things back down to the kitchen. I want you to change out of your clothes and take a good long shower. Can you do that for me?'

He nodded.

'Leave your clothes outside your bedroom door. OK?'

He didn't speak.

'Do you understand Daniel?'

'Y ...yes.'

'Did anyone see you in the alley?'

'I don't think so, no.'

'OK.'

I picked up the knife, lay it on the tea-tray and left him.

Using an old newspaper, I wrapped the knife, and secured the package with a handful of elastic bands. I could drive to the river later, to the point where it flowed the fastest. Watch the package be carried away downstream.

When I heard the shower running, I went back upstairs and gathered up the bloodied clothes into the linen basket. Ninety degrees was the hottest wash the machine would do. I emptied a box of stain remover into the detergent dispenser, and a cup of bleach. I sat in the utility room, watching the clothes rotate, seeing the scalding water and bleach remove all trace of Byron Reynolds.

Just like I sat here ten years ago, and watched the machine remove all traces of the bully that was Daniel's father, after that long and hideous custody battle.

No one will ever take my Daniel, my son, away from me. No one.

Tonia Bevins

ALIEN

She delves beneath the covers, purring,
finds the crook of foetal-folded knees.
How quickly she absents herself in dreams,
my alien familiar. Stretching on the morning,
she holds me in her haughty gaze.
Were I wolf I'd be her slave.

I am cast to please and serve –
a rude mechanical, tossed aside,
inconsequential as a spent mouse.
Now she'll freeze – then chase her aerial tail –
run mad, as if pursued by djinn,
distracted, breakneck, pinned-back ears
tuned to signals from an unseen world,
my familiar alien.

David H. Varley

AND IT'S MADNESS TIME AGAIN

Lines Written on the Calling of the 2017 General Election

And it's madness time again, you know,
A time for nationwide dejection –
Oh god, oh hell, oh Christ, oh no,
It's another bloody election!

Like Roman Caesar our Mother Theresa
Has suddenly gone St Joan,
And her Tory hordes are marching towards
A mandate all of her own.
So Davis and Fox are both laughing stocks,
And Boris a Bullingdon creep,
But what do you care? They're going nowhere,
And the price may be awfully steep.

There's that Islington prat with his beard and his hat,
And his friends in the IRA.
He's a pound-shop Trot who's certainly not
Going to blow anyone's mind away.
When McDonnell barks he's parroting Marx,
And Abbot wants Jew-hating men in.
If you like that shite, why take it lite?
I'd sooner vote for Lenin.

There's poor little Tim, quite pleasant but dim,
Full of sad Europeany frowns.
But even if Brexit both buggers and wrecks it,
The country won't vote in his clowns.
Even Vince Cable is completely unable
To distinguish this mob from the herd:
They'd take first place in a donkey race
But here they'll come in third.

Now UKIP, I think, are well on the brink,
And look like they're going for broke,
And the berk in the tweed did poorly indeed
At the hands of the people of Stoke.
But Nigel Farage is still horribly at large,
Mouthing off on TV with impunity,
And kissing the rump of the odious Trump
At every allowed opportunity.

But worst of all is the mad caterwaul
From that sour Caledonian trout:
'Och, Scotland forever, peace, love and whatever,
Unless you're English – get out!'
With the SNP, the issue for me
Is that goodwill for Britons is sparse.
When it's all about race, then I know my place –
I'm a hated Sassenach arse!

There's more beside, Welsh nitwits in Plaid,
And the Greens with their vacuous guff,
Over the sea, Sinn Fein, DUP,
In a mess of Hibernian stuff.
The whole bloody class should be put out to grass,
They're daft, they're mad, they're remote,
But oh what the hell, I do know full well,
...I'm still gonna trudge out to vote.

Helena Abblett

THE DAILY DALYAN

You should greet each hot, dusty day with a firm handshake
Give a deep smile and then say *Merhaba*.
But remember to not be like my Dad, who always says it
wrong.
You must put the emphasis on the first syllable
And sing *habaaa*, lazily but increasing in tone.

Unfortunately, I'm stuck if anyone tries to continue the
conversation.
Most Turkish people in Dalyan speak English though, so that's
OK.
Iztuzu is the beach, with a long shallow sea that is
Mediterranean blue.
Efes is the beer. *Serefe!* ('sair-uh-fay') says my Mum.
It's OK to drink beer every day in Dalyan.

Each day is segmented by the call to prayer,
Sung tirelessly from the mosque, which is situated in the centre
of town –
It's not far at all from the bars and restaurants
Despite Erdogan's (say 'erd-o-wan's') ban on sales within a
hundred yards,
A regular reminder that we are still in a Muslim country.

It's nice to take a lunchtime stroll down the main drag.
It has a Sports Direct, a JD Sports, and a Primark,
But of course it doesn't really,
You can buy a genuine fake whenever you want
'Just browsing?' I'm pleased the customer service is sincere

Except on market days
When you have to have your wits about you and my Dad gets
called 'Baldy'.
One bent old woman is a regular feature
Grabbing unwilling wrists to drape cheap bracelets on
And then demanding lira.

In the evening there is a lot of life in Dalyan –
Dogs out on the randan, cats pulling at old food spilling out of
bins.
Many revellers are at the end of their days, skin dark and
deeply furrowed by the sun.
Each night we see the white-haired lady at the Pop-in Fun Pub
Sitting with her beer, phone and young Turkish lover.

On a quiet day, take a walk to see the culture at Kaunos
Stand in the old Greek and Roman amphitheatre and ask, 'are
you not entertained?'
Centuries of civilisation have come to this, and I fear for my
own maiden, my Persephone.
Fag ends amongst the rock terraces and a magazine in my bag
Boasting an interview with a lady who injected concrete into
her arse.

It is almost time for bed in Dalyan.
My words are choked as I give my best wishes to Mum and
Dad.
The plane leaves at two in the morning
And they will stay behind for their twilight days.
I can't remember the Turkish word for goodbye.

Joan Dowling

GNOTHI SEAUTON

She slips her hand into mine. Startled, I turn to look at her.

'It's like Delphi!' she cries, eyes shining.

I follow her gaze. In the dawn stillness the heat haze shivers before parting to reveal steeply rolling hills. Fragile sunlight creeps down to the river far below.

It's fifty years since we climbed the Sacred Way but I see immediately what she means. High on Mount Parnassus we'd watched the sun rise through shredded morning mist. Our first view of the prophetic mountain slopes and hidden valleys held us spellbound. Around us, pilgrims seeking spiritual guidance explored the ancient myth of the Delphic Oracle. We rejoiced that we agreed on a chosen wisdom to guide us on our own shared path – the inscription on the Temple of Apollo – Gnothi Seauton: Know Thyself.

Now, as the sun starts to warm us, I feel again a sense of destiny. I'd chosen this place for its air of calm restfulness, the spirit of Delphi not apparent to me then. But had I chosen it unconsciously? Deluded myself that, here, we might find our way again?

A cloud conceals the sun and she becomes restless. I draw her close but she pulls away. Turning her face to mine, I see she's left me again; blank, resentful eyes stare back at me. She doesn't know herself – will never know herself again.

'Who are you?' she frets. 'I want to go home.'

I take her hand and lead her back inside.

Linda Leigh

EULOGY FOR A SANDWICH

Death comes to all of us and today is no exception as I bite firmly into my chargrilled chicken sandwich at Browns today to celebrate my birthday.

I felt sorry for the sandwich as I hungrily bit deep into the chargrilled bloomer and munched on my frites!

I did think about the chicken for a nanosecond, about how it was once a living animal, enjoying life, just like me today. I wondered if the chicken bit deep into its corn and what the corn thought when it was alive and had ears, before the plough cut short its young tender life, by slicing off its ears!

Back to my delicious lunch and a quick drink of my peach Bellini to wash the chicken down with – at least I was giving it a good send-off by enjoying a drink that would fizz, sparkle and light the way from my jaws into my soft floating inner tummy! Yummy!

I took my sandwich apart and noticed the chicken was well dressed for the occasion, with avocado and a cloak of green gem lettuce. What a star! Matches my birthstone emerald, but then it did like to strut its wares around the barn when alive and had a ball with the young chicks in there!

I wonder if chickens can think like us? Should I keep biting? No point worrying, it's dead now and its soul is floating above me, admiring how succulent her body still is, nestled deep inside my bloomer, despite death destroying its head with the swift fall of the axe!

If I die later today or tomorrow from food poisoning, then the chicken will still be with me and will have passed death to me Therefore my theory is confirmed: we live, we die, circles of life continue, we live again, somewhere else perhaps.

Nemma Wollenfang

CURIOSUS CATTUS

Curiosity overcame her. The shopping bag was there, lying open on the kitchen floor, with no human around to attend it. Any cat would be much remiss in their duties as the household inspector if they were to forgo an examination of its contents. Investigation, one could say, was obligatory.

Nose first, Tarro dove in. Bread – wholemeal. Eggs – a dozen. Milk – sealed tight. Drat. Newspaper – that would require shredding later. Tarro rooted further, loving the way the plastic crinkled beneath her paws. Sniff... sniff... Tomatoes, cabbage, melon...

Aha! Cat treats! And a lot of them!

Three whole packets.

Hmm. Treats, while appreciated, boded ill. The humans always bought them in abundance before 'that time of year'. You know the one. *The vet visit*. Ugh. Tarro shuddered at the mere thought. It was as if guilt drove them to it, as if her owners could somehow remedy the heinousness of their actions with a few measly crunchables! Not that they weren't delicious... In fact, they almost made the whole ordeal worthwhile... But it was the principle of the matter! Being manhandled into that tiny box, being jolted and jostled about and jabbed by the cruel vet. It was too much to be borne!

Which set Tarro to thinking... If there were no treats, perhaps... perhaps there would be no vet visit. Of course! Without those sweet morsels to cushion the blow, the humans would feel too *guilty* to take her. The plan was brilliant, pure genius! Diabolical, even. All Tarro had to do was dispose of them. But how? There was the obvious, but she could never consume them all by herself, not in time. The humans would likely return too soon for that...

The dog.

Nearby, Bongo slept soundly in his huge bed – tongue lolling, all fours in the air, one massive paw twitching. That daft mongrel was always getting himself into trouble. Just yesterday he'd smashed the mistress's favourite vase while bounding about the house like a loon. Adding another black mark to his name wouldn't make much of a difference. It would be *far* too easy.

So, one by one, Tarro carried the treat-packets over and stashed them behind his bed, daintily crinkling her nose against his canine stench. Bongo huffed once, snuffled, but slept on. Oblivious. With the final packet, Tarro, regretfully, sliced a claw down one side to release a trail of treats. Unfortunately, some must be sacrificed if this was to work. She left them in a pile beside Bongo. Then, to add to the effect, Tarro dragged over the newspaper too and gave it a thorough mauling.

Perfect. The scene of the crime was set.

Blaming the dog is standard practice – as every competent feline knows. And if no mutt is present within a household, then the toddler did it, of course.

'Bongo! Tarro! We're home!'

The humans!

Tarro made herself scarce, casually strolling into the hall via the lounge to greet the mistress and her husband, instead of the kitchen. She slunk about the former's legs.

'There you are, Tarro darling.'

A pair of arms reached down to sweep her up for mandatory cuddles. Hmm. She released a satisfied purr, fluffing the padding of her mistress's coat. Tarro, while not an ideal name, was at the very least short. Thus, she tolerated it. Name-tags were often large and cumbersome – she could not imagine having something longer emblazoned across her collar. The Persian down the street yoked a plaque half the size of his head!

Poor Commodore Valerian Fluffypaws…

She allowed the human to carry her through the house, calling for Bongo as she went. Upon entering the kitchen her mistress stopped and gasped. 'Oh, Bongo! No!'

Half-awake, the hound had apparently toppled out of bed upon hearing the mistress's call and fallen, face-first, into the pile of treats. Now, he was squinting down at them with a truly dumfounded expression.

'Have you seen this, James?!' the mistress screeched. 'Bongo stole Tarro's treats. *And* he's destroyed the newspaper! Bad dog, bad *bad* Bongo!'

Bongo dipped his head, looking suitably chastised, and wrapped his tail around his haunches. Ah, what a pleasant sight. The dog, humiliated. Tarro adopted her 'Shame on you, Bongo' face too, for good measure. It wasn't the first time she'd worn it.

'I've told you before not to leave the shopping on the floor, dear,' the husband said. 'Even while just nipping next door. You know what he's like. Bongo can't help himself, the big lug.'

He ruffled the canine's ear affectionately.

'But we can't take Tarro to the *you-know-what* without her treats,' the mistress said, sounding utterly distressed. 'We just can't. It's hard enough as it is on the poor dear. What are we going to do?'

Yes, Tarro mused, *what indeed?*

It was much later, as Tarro was reclining in her heated bed musing on her own brilliance, that a mouth-watering scent piqued her interest. Meaty, moreish. Nostrils flaring, her eyes snapped open to see her smiling mistress crouched before her with a… Yes! Her nose had not lied. Fried chicken!

'For you, my darling.' She set the plate down.

Tarro didn't hesitate, she just dug in. Succulent, tender, juicy. Hmm, marvellous. It had been cooked in butter, she could tell by that delightfully creamy aftertaste. Ah, purrrfection.

She'd barely swallowed her last mouthful and was just setting about the task of licking the plate clean, when a hand scooped her up and she was tumbling backwards into a dark, shadowy space.

What the?! A cage! Oh no. Its barred door snapped shut.

'I'm sorry, Tarro,' the mistress smiled sadly. 'I really am but you need your shots.'

Tarro released a yowl as the box was hefted up, making it as pitiful as she could, but it did no good. The mistress would not relent. Soon they were out the door and into the car, with the engine humming to life. That was when Tarro gave up and huffed, completely put out.

Her plan had been foiled.

Winner of the Northwich LitFest Short Story Competition 2017
Previously published in Ourtown Magazine.

Shantele Janes

HAD YOU STAYED

Some days when I wake
I forget –
precious seconds of amnesia.

I pray for those mornings,
would give up whole weeks
in exchange for a moment
of a world
where I do not have to remember
the emptiness of life
without you.

I named you
a million times over,
Rachael for a girl,
Toby for a boy,
while you lay
in my swollen belly,
just a flutter
a heartbeat of hope.

Even then
I could picture
my face in yours,
like the moon
casts its reflection
on the sea.

How I wanted to hold you,
to bury my nose in your neck
and breathe you in,
blow raspberries on your belly
and make you giggle.

How I longed to see
whether your eyes were
blue or green,
to look into them
and to know you.

I still crave to be woken
by your cry,
to know what that sounds like,
to be able to cradle you in the night,
soothe your tears
and sing you lullabies.

Now I chase sleep
to dream of you,
of what was
and what could have been,
had you stayed
with me.

Gwili Lewis

PERFECT DRIVER ODE

If you can keep your head when drivers all about you
Lose their tempers and blame it on to you;
If you can trust your driving skill when others doubt you
But make allowance for their doubting too;
If you can cause a traffic jam, yet not be weary
Of wearying rude remarks of others on the road,
And in the face of hatred, your smile is cheery
To those who hate and your patience goad.

If you can dream and not make dreams your master
Thinking you're the greatest driver of them all,
With skill to avoid a motorway disaster,
Horrendous pile-up and a carnage to appall.
If you can hold your tongue as others pass you
At speed on winding double white lines;
If patient you can be when juggernauts tail you,
And silent, 'stead of calling other drivers 'swines'.

If you can drive with crowds and keep your distance
From him in front, and not accelerate when fools cut in;
If you can dip your lights, humbly, and show no arrogance,
If others count and not be hurt by one motoring sin;
If you can drive faultlessly every minute
With care no matter what's the mileage done;
Yours is the earth and everything that's in it;
And what is more, you'll be a *freak* my son.

Published in the spring 2017 issue of Evergreen magazine
www.evergreenmagazine.co.uk

Steven Capstick

SPIRIT OF THE NIGHT

The car door slams and her dress sways in the gentle breeze; she gives a cursory wave and hurries towards the marquee. Pretty girls, dressed to party, greet her. They all raise their hands and chorus a collective squeal. I sit at the wheel of my father's car and watch them; watch her. She doesn't know but she's been my heart's desire from the age of nine. She bewitches me but I have never told her that I see her inner grace and beauty.

There is the smell of roses on the wind and magic sparkles under the lights. Music plays for the dancers and the lovers but not for the lonely dream people. It's later when she leaves the marquee to stand on the lawn, alone. The other girls have melted away. I can see in her face she hates the clothes, the hair and make-up. A boy, beer bottle in hand stands inside, calling out to her, laughing.

She's running now, her dress bedraggled and stained. I know she is destined to roam broken-hearted down the years. If I could take one moment in my hands, it would be this one. I'd pick her up, take her for a ride, turn this corner and just keep going, never looking back. Suddenly I hear a voice, distant, calling me home but on that soft, infected summer night I follow the boy as he leaves.

Down at the river I fight with Jimmy until his blade leaves a gaping hole in me and my soul. Remembering this makes my eyes go dark and my blood run cold. The street lights grow dim as I try to focus on her smiling face. Each time I return to this scene, I can never explain why I didn't ask her to that prom.

Debbie Bennett

TEN TO NINE

Ten minutes before the school bell.

'Are we there yet?'

'Ten minutes.'

'You said that last time, Mum. Didn't she say that last time, Carly? How can it still be ten minutes, if it was ten minutes five minutes ago? Unless school's got further away than it was before. Do you think school's moving, Carly? Why are you poking a stick in your eye, Carly? Carly, why—'

'Shut *up*, pigface.'

'Mum, Carly called me pigface. Did you hear her? I don't have a pig's face, do I, Mum?'

'Josh, stop annoying your sister. Carly, don't put mascara on in the car. If I have to stop suddenly, you'll lose an eye.'

'Then don't stop suddenly.'

Teenagers. Being a hands-on parent wasn't how Lyn had imagined her life at all. Not that she didn't love the little brats, it was just that driving a stroppy fourteen-year-old and her irritating eight-year-old brother to school hadn't exactly been on her roadmap. Her forties were supposed to be about climbing the career ladder, breaking the glass ceiling and all the other clichés that had gone out the window when she'd got made redundant two years ago and they'd had to let the nanny go. She missed her company car – with only two seats, the kids couldn't both fit in it and it was so much more peaceful than this great big tank of a 4-wheel drive.

They were late again this morning. Josh wouldn't eat his breakfast without watching CBBC, Carly needed to spend at least twenty minutes straightening her hair and they'd stopped at the village shop for lunch stuff, where the kids had to choose from the small range available and while Carly wouldn't eat meat, Josh wouldn't eat anything at all unless it was crammed full of E numbers. Ah well – by the time she picked them up, he'd have worn off the hyperactivity in the school playground.

'Lyn, did you wash my top?'

'Which top, Carly?'

'The black one. The one I told you I wanted for tomorrow.'

Damn. Lyn wondered if she could put the top back on Carly's bedroom floor and pretend it had been there all along.

'Are we there yet?'

'Did you wash my *top?*'

'Don't shout. I'll sort your top out later. Now who can be the first to spot a yellow car?'

Nine cars in front of her at the traffic lights. Lyn tapped her fingers on the steering wheel as Carly's mobile phone beeped with yet another text message. They weren't even her kids, not really – she hadn't had nine months of carrying each of them around to get used to the idea of being a parent. No, they'd come as a package deal with their father six years ago. *Three for the price of one,* he'd announced, and while it had seemed like a bargain at the time, she hadn't counted on the year-on-year increase in cost – time, money, *effort* – and for what? To be spoken to by a sulky teenager like she was no more than the housekeeper-cum-chauffeur?

Somewhere up in front there was a commotion and the sound of sirens. Down the High Street an engine backfired – once, twice – and the traffic lights changed to green. The car crawled forwards and they would have made it through the junction, had it not been for the stupid woman in the red mini in front, who stalled, restarted the engine and then jumped the lights on amber.

'We're going to be late. Again,' said Carly.

'Are we there yet?' Josh squirmed on his booster seat. 'Why is there a policeman with a gun over there?'

'Don't be silly, Josh.' Lyn wondered what excuse she could give the school this time.

'But there *is* a policeman. And he *has* got a gun.'

31

Carly looked up from her mobile. 'For once the little shit is right.'

'*Carly!* I do *not* want to hear—' She broke off as she saw the armed police officer across the junction. He was looking directly at her.

Eight seconds and the lights changed to green, but before Lyn had a chance to react, the passenger door of the car flew open and a man leapt in, slammed the door and yelled 'Drive!'

Lyn had the vague impression of a youth in a navy-blue sweatshirt and jeans, but it was the knife in his hands – his bloody hands – and the policeman's gun pointing at the car that bypassed the rational part of her brain, and she slammed her foot onto the accelerator and screeched away from the junction.

'Onto the ring road.'

'What?'

'Get onto the ring road. Out of town. I don't care – just drive.'

Lyn glanced into the mirror to see a wide-eyed Josh and Carly looking back at her. She took the nearside lane up to the ring road. 'What did you do?' she asked, surprised how calm she sounded.

'Nothing. But Rob shot—' He held up the knife, blood dripped onto the seat and both Carly and Josh shrieked.

The youth clapped his hands over his ears, clearly not used to screaming children, but the knife wavered perilously close to Lyn's head.

Carly stopped screaming. In the mirror, Lyn saw her turn to her brother. 'Shut up. Don't speak. Just *listen*. We have to do what he says.'

'But—' Josh hiccupped and shut up.

Lyn returned her attention to their passenger, who was still holding the knife out. 'Would you mind putting that down?' she asked.

'Can't. I need you to drive to Manchester. On the motorway. Or I'll kill the boy.'

'Good idea,' said Carly from the back. There was no trace of the terror from the scream a few seconds earlier. 'Stick the knife in him. He's a pain in the arse.'

Seven miles to the M56. Once they got to the motorway, Lyn knew they'd be harder to find. She wondered if the police helicopter was up yet and how they'd spot her. Sneaking a sideways look, she realised her passenger was barely more than a child, not yet shaving, and his free hand was clutching his stomach.

'It's your blood, isn't it?'

He nodded. 'Rob shot me. He shot the security guard and one of the bullets hit me.'

'Does it hurt?' Carly leaned forwards. 'I watch *Casualty*,' she added. 'On TV. Did you rob a bank? That's *cool*. What's your name?'

'You don't need to know.'

But Carly wasn't giving up. 'No, but since we're here and you're about to murder my little brother, it'd be nice to know your name.'

Josh made a strange noise. 'It's Tom, OK? Now shut up.'

'Hi, Tom. My name's Carly Johnson. My step-mum is Lyn. Where are we, anyway?'

'On the A56,' said Lyn.

Six long minutes. No sirens, no sound of a helicopter. Just Carly chattering incessantly, reading out road signs and asking where they were. Normally it was Josh who provided the soundtrack to their lives with constant repetition and questions, but now Josh was staring out of the window in silence and Lyn had a sneaking suspicion that he'd wet himself – there was a hint of ammonia above the coppery smell of blood – and yet Carly hadn't mentioned it and she'd normally pounce on any opportunity to humiliate her brother.

She was taking the long route to the motorway; the lack of comment confirmed her idea that the boy wasn't a local and had no real idea of where they were. He was so *young*, caught up in something that was out of control and Lyn felt sorry for him, wondering who this Rob was who had let him down so badly.

'Shall we stop and I'll look at your wound?' she asked, when Carly let her get a word in. It was unlike her step-daughter to be so talkative; at weekends she sometimes never got past a grunt.

'No.'

'You're hurt.'

'No! Shut up all of you and let me *think*.'

Five people in a line on the motorway junction bridge, a police car and a van parked behind them. Lyn had been driving east on the motorway for a few miles now and surely they were watching out for her?

'Are we on the M56 now, Mum?'

'Yes.' Carly never called her mum. Josh did – he'd been so young, he probably didn't even remember his real mother, but Carly had been a harder nut to crack and Lyn hadn't forced the issue.

'Where are we heading?'

'Towards Manchester.' She bit back a gasp as she saw a flash of blue accelerating down the slip road onto the motorway behind them.

Four heartbeats – she felt every one. The boy turned around in his seat. 'Shit!'

'They're only three cars behind us, Mum,' said Carly, helpfully stating the obvious. 'And look at that big Sainsbury's lorry just ahead.'

What was she talking about? And why so loudly? Lyn looked in the mirror and the police car was almost on them now; it overtook and pulled in tight in front, the message board telling her to stop. Right now.

The boy raised the knife again, but he was clearly in pain.

Lyn signalled and moved onto the hard shoulder before slowing to a halt.

Three armed police officers piled out of the car.

Lyn turned to the boy. 'It's over,' she said gently. 'Give me the knife; you haven't hurt us.'

'I *can't*. They'll send me away.' He was crying now as he twisted and grabbed Carly's wrist. Something fell to the floor in the back of the car.

Carly whimpered.

Two kids, who she loved very much. Would always love.

An armed officer opened one of the rear doors and grabbed a startled Josh. Carly pulled her hand away and scrambled after him.

Another officer ripped open the passenger door and yelled at the boy. He tried to get up but fell out of the car onto the grass verge.

Lyn heard a sound from the back of the car. A voice.

One mobile phone with an open connection. Lyn picked it up, held it to her ear and heard the operator at the other end.

'The police should be with you now.'

Joyce Ireland

THE KINDNESS OF A STRANGER

Hannah pulled the shawl round her thin shoulders and closed the front door behind her. She was due to see Mr Earle in an hour or so, after the midday church bell. The wind blew cold and she had to watch where she walked to avoid the ice on the rutted lane.

The normally easy walk through the village to the manor house seemed hard in her present weak state. However, she knew that if her children were to be properly clothed this winter she needed to plead for help from Part's charity. Mr Earle was the chairman of the trustees and was known for his ability to listen sympathetically to supplicants.

The meeting had gone well and it was with great relief that Hannah took her leave and set off for home. She had Mr Earle's promise to present her case to the Board of Trustees at the forthcoming meeting.

As she crossed the Market Square and into Church Lane, the wind began to rise and she felt the cold through the whole of her body. She began to feel rather dizzy and somewhat disoriented. She tried to fix her sights on the Cross Keys Inn and the village hall at the top of Common Lane.

Suddenly, she was aware of a strange thundering noise and what appeared to be a bright light coming from along the High Street. She stumbled and, falling forward, seemed to spin through the beam of the light into darkness.

When Hannah opened her eyes, she struggled to rise but strong hands held her.

'What is happening? John, where are you?'

A strange man looked down at her. He was no one she knew but he appeared to be trying to help her. He looked puzzled and asked, 'Who are you? How do you know my name?'

As she roused from the faint, she noticed he was wearing a strange uniform, not military so far as she could tell, but of dark material with bright buttons and a badge with the letters L.C.T. in red and gold on it.

'I must get home to John and the children.' She looked around frantically. The stranger shrugged off his jacket and covered her. He helped her to sit up and, asking her to remain still for a moment, he disappeared. When he returned he offered her a warm sweet drink from a cup of unfamiliar light material. She drank deeply then struggled to her feet.

'Let me help you. Do you live near here?' the man asked.

She pointed down the lane. 'At the end there. I must get home; my children are so hungry.'

He disappeared again and returning, offered her a packet wrapped in shiny paper. 'Go on, love. You look as though you could do with some food. They're only cheese and corned beef. I can get something at the chippy later.'

Hannah didn't understand all of this but she accepted gratefully. 'Sir, you are mightily kind and I thank you.' She smiled at him.

He took her arm and supported her as she indicated the way. They walked past the inn and the hall and came to a terrace of cottages. Hannah turned into No. 3 and looked back to thank her benefactor. There was no sign of him, only the frozen duck pond and the green with its sprinkling of snow. After the brightness of the strange light, the afternoon was once more dark. She still held the shiny package.

Liz Leech

PRESERVED

Dark glossy berries, ripe and juicy,
Glistening in the late summer sunlight.
Sweet as sweet.
Juice stained my fingers,
Thorns nicked my skin
And the biggest berries hung
Temptingly just out of reach.

Insects tiptoed over the fruit,
Sucking up the over ripe juices,
Purple spillage over dark green leaves.
Others buzzed about their business
Where yellow pollen dusted
The few remaining bramble flowers
'Ere, as legend has it,
Witches shrivel the fruit
At the onset of autumn.

Apples are released from the bough,
Nudged before their time,
Marred by the coddling moth,
Or pecked by impatient birds
Testing their sweetness.
They drop to the ground,
Bounce and settle amongst the nettles.
Pale brown bruises spread like fungi
To scar their dappled beauty.

Small rodents scurry over to gnaw greedily,
Their eyes round as berry pebbles,
Searching for predators in the dusk.
Their fur twitches,
Legs and tail primed for flight
At the slightest hint of danger.

And when they are gone,
Slugs move ponderously through the grasses,
Extending and contracting their way
Towards the fruit,
Little greedy eyes on stalks
Waving to and fro.

All help themselves
To autumn's abundance –
And I would join the fray.
Jelly was trapped in jars
As I was trapped in the kitchen,
Brought out and exhibited
When someone came to tea.

Marian Smith

FINDING LEO

I found your name carved in stone
Over the schoolhouse door.
A name I knew, a distant branch of the family tree,
Severed, still green.

Sometimes I can see you.
You are grinning, with tobacco teeth, macassar hair
You smell of sweat and beer and the weaving shed.
You are seventeen. And immortal.

What did you dream of, on some dark November day in the
Clarence Mill,
When the looms roared and the shuttles crashed like machine
gun fire?
Were you playing centre forward for Macclesfield,
Kissing Elsie from Chapel Street?

I found your name in print
Between Sapper Howe and Corporal Arden (both wounded).
Leo, son of Peter and Mary
Killed in France. Age 19.

And I want to ask you:
Did three years in the Clarence Mill
Deaden the sound of the gunfire?

You have no grave,
But I found your name buried
On page 74 of *Soldiers Who Died in the Great War*
Volume 27.

You are lost in time
But I want to see you.
Not sobbing, trapped on wire
Flesh torn from splintered bone

But grinning, with tobacco teeth, macassar hair
You smell of sweat and beer and the weaving shed
You are seventeen and immortal
And the mill is for life and the Somme is just a river.

In memory of Leo Mattimore
Born Bollington, Cheshire February 1897
Died Gommecourt, France, July 1916

Les Green

OMINOUS

I'm usually a positive person. I have such a positive outlook, that the negative thought stands out like a black mark on freshly laundered linen. And at the moment I don't even know what it means yet. But I'm convinced it means something because I have good instincts and I've learned to trust them.

I'm sure you've experienced something similar, where you instinctively know something without realising it. Somewhere in your brain, you've been receiving indicators and information. Body language, a turn of phrase, one excuse too many. You know, that kind of thing. Without realising it, your supercomputer is putting all the pieces together without you making any effort to acknowledge or understand it. Then suddenly your brain finishes the calculation and serves you up a fully formed thing that you absolutely know without a shadow of a doubt.

Something is up with my computer at the moment. I shouldn't be aware of the process but I am. I know just enough to know that it's working on something and it sits in the pit of my stomach like a wrecking ball waiting to swing. Only now that I know there's a something, it's impossible to just look the other way and let my brain get on with it and serve me up the result. So it's 2am when I write this, and I have the stupid idea that I'll try and distract my brain by giving it something else to do, but all thoughts turn to this thing – this ominous thing.

I can imagine my life as being constructed of fine delicate objects, built and stacked up on delicate shelves like a glass menagerie. When it's sunny – and it usually is sunny where I sit – the light hits every surface and fills me up. Every corner is illuminated and nothing is left in darkness. Except now I realise how fragile it all is. The glass feels like it's ready to go. I can feel this ominous thing rolling on the surface, making that solid, deep, purposeful scratch you get from a glass cutter. Something deliberate and inevitable. This isn't an accident. Nobody died or got pregnant or forgot to buy the winning lottery ticket. This is related to choice. Somebody decided to do something and I can feel them dragging the glass cutter across my life. A lever is being pulled and a wheel is turning in their life and it's going to have a negative impact on mine.

So here I am, past 2am on a Tuesday morning and waiting for the ominous thing to reveal itself. Most of me really doesn't want to know what it is but Mr Logical wants it to get out in the open so he can see it and poke it with a stick. I just want it to be done and the aftershock to be over. I want the wrecking ball to stop swinging. I want to see the end of this thing. This ominous thing.

Shauna Leishman

MOMENTS

The truth is, our lives are made up of moments –
moments strung together, sometimes linked only by time
creating a mood, an event, an existence.
Perhaps accomplishing something one can see.
Perhaps not.

Moments of joy and despair,
creation and letting go,
acquiring and giving,
enduring and getting through
Moments sitting in silence,
Moments of pushing through a crowd.

Moments spent sitting in a darkening room
on a winter's afternoon,
warm mug of tea, cat curled on lap,
Chopin nocturnes filling the air.

Moments spent wrestling a ballet costume
onto a wriggly three-year-old,
in a crowded, cold clubhouse,
moms in similar pose on every side.

Moments at a convivial dinner party,
stories from gentle people
of childhood rejections and accumulated sorrows,
recent travel adventures and hometown oppressions,
unexpected dog rescues and turtles on beaches.

Moments of giving birth –
to a baby
to a marriage
to an idea made manifest
to a success
to a new friendship

Moments of dying:
to lose abilities hard earned,
to lose strength,
to endure pain,
to lose someone, or everyone.

Moments of learning:
how to walk, how to read,
to drive, or a new skill,
how to play, how to work,
when to sit still, when to light a fire,
how to comfort, how to fight a wrong.

Moments of just being –
maybe in tears, maybe awestruck,
doing nothing – but somehow your presence
brings a meaning to a life, to a world, to a purpose.

Sometimes we fear moments will last forever.
But they never do.
It can just feel that way.
Sometimes we wish moments could last forever.
But they never do
We get to keep the memories.

Moments – you can't take them or leave them.
They just keep relentlessly rolling along –
cruel, merciful, full, empty, forever –
building a life
over and over and over again.

David Bruce

THE VENGEFUL SHAWL

The men of Inglesport had long abandoned their fishing and taken to piracy. But even then these craven villains could not face cold-blooded murder. They'd make their victims walk the plank and then pretend they'd had nothing to do with their drowning.

When they captured the schooner *The Bewitched*, they made everyone walk the plank, even the captain's wife. But as the prick of rapier forced her along the plank, a pirate noticed the beautiful silk shawl she was wearing and clawed it from her shoulders just as she was falling into the sea below. The shawl would make a good present for Sadie, his woman ashore.

That evening as Sadie was dressing for the celebrations that always followed a successful raid, she stopped in front of the newly acquired mirror to admire her shawl's bright colours and pretty pattern. A mirror that just happened to have been plundered from the cabin of that very same captain's wife from whom the shawl had been taken. Sadie swayed this way and that, admiring herself in the pier glass, but another image began to emerge from deep within its depths. The bulging eyes and grey wasted face of a woman expanded, solidified and came to rest upon her shoulder as an accusing finger rose to point at the shawl. Sadie was helpless in horror as the shawl rose up from her neck to cover her head and face and then coiled itself tight around her neck. Tighter and tighter it wound itself and no amount of clawing could free it until all life had left her body.

Her partner had heard the choking sounds and hurried into the room only to find his woman blue in the face and dead on the floor with the shawl lying innocently alongside her. Everyone assumed it was some kind of natural tragedy, a seizure of some kind.

There was a big following at the funeral and the shawl was placed in the back of a cupboard.

In a short space of time the pirate had moved another woman into the cottage with him. Eager to make it her own home, as women will, she set about sorting out the drawers and cupboards and found the beautiful silk shawl in the back of one of them. She quickly took ownership and added it to her store of fineries.

Alone in the house one day, she dressed and put the shawl about her shoulders to pose in front of the mirror to admire herself, as ladies sometimes do. Soon she saw alongside her own face another image, that bleached-out face of a drowned woman. The shawl rose up and inexorably coiled itself around her neck until she too was quite dead. The shawl fell innocently alongside her.

The pirate returned to the house to find his latest woman blue in the face and lying dead upon the floor, just like her predecessor. Some thought it was a seizure, but others were not so sure.

Fewer attended the funeral this time. The silk shawl was placed in the back of a drawer.

Time passed and the pirate found himself with yet another woman brave enough to move in with him. Once settled in, she too began to sort out the household, as women do, and found that seductive silk shawl in the back of the drawer and she added it to her drawer-full of fripperies.

The following Saturday whilst dressing for the dance, she took out the shawl and posed in front of the mirror to admire herself, as women often do. But there was another reflection in the glass – that pale hypnotic face of the captain's drowned wife with her hollowed cheeks and seaweed in her hair.

The shawl rose up and coiled itself serpent-like around her neck until all life had left her body and then it fell innocently to the floor.

The pirate came into the room to find his latest woman lying blue of face and dead upon the floor.

No one thought it was a seizure.

That evening the woman's brothers led a large angry mob to the cottage, shouting accusations and banging on the door. Fearing the worst, the pirate collected together his few valuables. Six gold coins, an ancient pistol, his tinderbox and then his eye caught the sight of the valuable silk shawl lying alongside the mirror. He flung it over his shoulders, but as he turned he happened to glimpse his image in the mirror. Another face – one he recognized – was staring out at him. Riveted to the spot, his eyes filled with fear. A bony finger pointed. The shawl rose up and tightened around his neck.

When the mob forced their way into the house, they found him on the floor, swathed in the shawl and quite dead. They left his body wrapped in the shawl and carried it to the clifftop and hurled it into the sea.

The body sank swiftly, but the shawl unwound and floated up onto the surface before slowly sliding below the welcoming waves.

Some say it was just the nature of the thing that it floated and then sank, but others who had been watching more closely say they saw a lady's hand rise up from the waves and drag her shawl back down into the deep.

Linda Leigh

12ᵀᴴ CENTURY FRANCE IN 2016

Walk up the hill.
Step back eight hundred years.
Wear your loin cloth and leather sandals.
Brush out the straw floors.
Stroke chestnut-coloured horses, waiting to race.

Polish your armour until it shines like a new pin, mirror finish.
Remove severed links and repair the heavy chain link dress.
Put on your helmet, pick up your sword and touch the
sharpness.

Ride fast with the wind in your face, down cobbled stone
streets,
Past the bell tower,
Under the arches,
Across green valleys,
Ride on. Don't stop.

Death sends a message –
Your soul responds to its call.
The castle looms up high above the rising mist.
Rickety wooden steps scale dizzy heights.
The trebuchet waits in silence,
Cannon balls at its feet.

Liz Sandbach

AT JODRELL BANK

We lay down together on the grass
beneath the great white dish
and contemplated the universe.
'Does the moon have a name?' you asked.
'Luna,' I said. 'It's Luna.'
'Oh, that's a pretty name.
And can a moon have a moon?'
'I don't know – good question.'
'So what's the strongest thing in the universe?'
'Love,' I said. 'It's love.'
You stretched out your hand and stroked my face.
'I love you,' I said.
And the great white dish stirred.
'I love you too –
all the way to the moon.'
We smiled
and the universe smiled back.

Joan Dowling

TALES OF THE UNEXPECTED

'Can you get that, Matt? I'm just going to check on the baby.'

As Jess ran lightly up the stairs, she heard her husband opening the door into the front hall. She glanced at her watch. 7.15pm seemed a bit late for unexpected callers.

Ben's bedroom was bathed in a warm, cosy glow from the small lamp beside his cot. She closed the door softly behind her and tiptoed across the room. Leaning forward, she gently stroked Ben's sleeping face. After six weeks, she was still in awe of the miracle that was her small son and she caught her breath as he stirred and sighed. Behind her, the door opened and Ben frowned and waved his tiny fists, as the light from the landing fell across his cot. Jess turned and motioned for Matt to close the door, but instead he beckoned her to join him outside. Reluctantly, she gave Ben a last lingering look, then followed Matt.

'What is it?' she kept her voice low.

'That ring on the doorbell.'

She'd already forgotten about that.

'It's Jamie and Alice.'

Her brow furrowed as she searched for clues.

Matt looked exasperated. 'That couple we met on holiday. Remember that we told them to drop in if ever they were in the area? They've dropped in.'

'At this hour? It's not exactly convenient. And not exactly good manners, either,' Jess added, with some annoyance. 'We hardly know them.'

'I know.' Matt's response was rueful. 'But what can we do? They seem anxious to see us.'

Together, they went downstairs and into the living room. As they entered, the vaguely familiar couple got to their feet, smiling.

'We thought we'd surprise you.' Alice came forward to

embrace Jess. 'We're on our way to visit my family in Scotland and we found ourselves only a couple of miles away from you. We remembered your invitation and decided to call in.'

Jess cast a fleeting, regretful look towards the kitchen, where she knew dinner would be nearly ready, then she turned back to her guests.

'It's good to see you both again. Can we offer you a drink?'

Jamie butted in excitedly. ' No, wait! Tell them our news first, Alice.' He beamed proudly at his wife, who looked down shyly. When she raised her eyes again, they were shining with tears.

'It's happened at last,' she whispered. 'We're going to have a baby!'

Then Jess remembered. When they met at the holiday hotel in Greece, they had got into conversation on that very first night over dinner and they seemed to get on well, so they dined together each evening after that. Jess had been blooming at that time, her pregnancy was just becoming noticeable and she attracted affectionate glances and congratulatory comments wherever she went. Alice was especially complimentary and solicitous, always ensuring that Jess was comfortable and taken care of. It wasn't until the last night that she confided to Jess that she and Jamie had been trying for several years for a child of their own. Jess's heart had gone out to her. Feeling guilty that her own happiness had prevented her from noticing Alice's sadness, she'd held her while she cried and told her how much she hoped that one day things would change and her turn would come.

And now it had. Genuinely delighted for her new friend, Jess held out her arms to Alice.

'That's wonderful news!' she cried, hugging her warmly.

Behind them, Matt and Jamie were laughing and shaking hands and, when she heard someone mention Champagne, she made a sudden decision.

'You must stay and eat with us. I'm not preparing anything very grand but I'm sure it's enough for us all.' She ignored the guarded look Matt gave her. 'You've got a long drive ahead of you and you'll need something to eat. We can swap baby notes over dinner.'

Dismissing their protestations and ignoring Matt's warning glance, Jess headed towards the kitchen to rescue the meal. 'Perhaps you'd like to freshen up, Alice? Top of the stairs, first left. But please don't waken Ben, it will be time for his feed soon.'

'Thank you, Jess.' Alice picked up her bag. 'You know only too well what we pregnant women are like!'

'I'll just go and get that bottle of Champagne out of the car. Our contribution,' Jamie told Matt. 'We've brought plenty to share with the relatives, they won't miss one bottle.'

Jess went into the kitchen, where Matt joined her.

'What's the matter with you?' she hissed. 'This is a huge thing for them. The least we can do is help to celebrate their good news.'

'Jess, it's an awful long way to Scotland, they've got hours of travelling to do yet. And now Jamie's getting Champagne. Don't you think they want us to offer them a bed for the night? It's a bit suspicious that they've called in so late. I think they were expecting to stay.'

'I hadn't thought of that,' Jess admitted, considering. 'Look, if the worst comes to the worst, the spare bed is already made up for your parents, so it wouldn't be too much trouble for one night, would it? Can't we just go with the flow?' She smiled persuasively at Matt.

He laughed, shaking his head, then opened the double doors leading into the next room. 'You win. I'd better get the dining room table ready, then.'

Jess hummed happily as she opened the fridge and unloaded lettuce, tomatoes, peppers. She felt so blessed to have Ben in her life, she couldn't help feeling excited for Alice and Jamie.

Suddenly remembering her hostess duties, she went back to check on her guests and found the front door ajar. She smiled as she looked out, half expecting to see Jamie lugging a suitcase from their car. For a fraction of a second, she froze. Then she raced for the stairs, screaming to Matt as she ran. But it was too late. The cot was empty.

Gwili Lewis

DAI THE DIDDLER

They called him Dai the Diddler
He kept the corner shop;
The way he diddled kindly folk
Was a scandal. It had to stop.

A cunning, devious chap was Dai,
Up to all sorts of tricks
To gain that extra bob or two,
But at last he was put in a fix.

A dear old soul went into his shop,
Her sister had come to stay;
She had a hunch, a chicken for lunch,
A treat for her guest, come what may.

'I won't be a jot, I'll see what I've got'
Said Dai to her standing there.
He knew he had one, and only that one
As he turned with an arrogant air.

And soon he was back, gave the chicken a smack,
Saying 'THIS is the fresh one for you.
It's just the ticket, it won't rob your pocket,
It's ideal, just the job for you two.'

She said not a word, but stared at the bird
As on its size she did ponder.
'I'm glad I did call…but it looks a bit small.
Slightly bigger I'd like. What's yonder?'

Dai picked up the bird, and said not a word,
But thought what to do next.
An idea he had, it was really quite bad.
He smirked and was not at all vexed.

Now when out of sight, sure he'd put things right
In a way that only Dai knew.
The diddling old jerk, on the bird set to work,
And the soul in the shop had no clue.

He tugged at the wings, pulled at the legs,
Blew it up to make it look bigger.
He thought it looked good, and buy it she should
The chicken he tried to transfigure.

Then back to the counter, at top speed went Dai
With the chicken, and a great big smile;
He showed her the bird, and said not a word.
His green eyes were so full of guile.

The dear old soul stood wondering there,
Pondering what's the best to do …
'I've made up my mind. If you be so kind,
I'll be happy to take home the two.'

Mac Carding

HOW MANY ON THE BOAT?

The rain was bouncing up from the coping stones like glass beads.

'How many people are on the boat?' the lock keeper at Dutton asked again.

'One,' mumbled Colin.

'We have to keep records, you see.'

The sun had been so hot last week that the grass was parched and brown. Down at Marsh Lock, Colin and Susan had been blackberrying and watching sunsets over the Mersey Estuary with their boat tied up against the old stone wall.

Stretching out into the Ship Canal, the ancient wooden pier rotted away gently.

'Let's see how far along we can go,' Susan had insisted.

'You're mad.' Colin had no head for heights or desire for adventuring.

She jumped over onto the first stanchion. Then it was an easy scramble right out over the water, clambering over missing planks and crawling along the baulks of timber where the deck was missing altogether.

Sitting at the very end of the pier, she watched as the curling, muddy water of the old Weaver estuary met the deep clearer water of the Manchester Ship Canal, with the sun beating down on her head. In the distance she could see a ship coming.

The hot afternoon sun shone on and reluctantly Susan decided she needed to move. The splintery wood was digging into the back of her thighs and she was getting cramp. When she moved, she lost her balance and fell in.

Colin was reading on the boat, completely unaware, so by the time he came looking for Susan there was no sign of her at all. Frantic with worry he called the police and they called the coastguard, but there was no search, no drama, no more Susan and Colin.

Susan was heading out into the Irish Sea, laughing in the wheelhouse with the Dutch captain.

David H. Varley

A GRAND TOUR

Hello everyone! Can I say how wonderful it is to see so many people turning out for the Plodsbury Historical Walkaround Tour! What's that? You're queuing for the bank? You too, madam? Oh. So who's actually here for the tour? Just you, sir? Fine. Fine. We may as well be on our way then, if you'll just follow me, sir.

Plodsbury is one of the great cultural centres of Britain, and is sometimes known as the 'Milan of East Anglia'. In fact, you may even hear Milan being described as the 'Plodsbury of North Italy'. What's that? You've never heard it called that before? Well, you have now.

The name of the town is believed to derive from that of a Saxon chieftain, Ploddo the Unpleasant, famed throughout the Germanic tribes for his unrivalled collection of venereal diseases. Ploddo was one of the earliest converts to Christianity in these isles, and a great missionary who personally beheaded over two hundred heathens who did not accept the love and mercy of Jesus Christ. He is commemorated by a plaque on the public convenience on this corner here, which is believed to be over his burial site.

The next historical mention of Plodsbury is in the Domesday Book, which records 'a diseased cesspit of little coin and much dirt'. Modern historians like myself, however, believe that this cannot be an accurate description of what was surely even then a vibrant economic centre, and the theory therefore is that this entry may be the earliest example of tax evasion in European history.

Plodsbury's status as a major cultural town was well established by the end of the Middle Ages, including even getting a flattering mention as the home of one of the pilgrims in Chaucer's *Canterbury Tales*. Sorry? You don't remember that?

Well, the reference is only found in one manuscript, the so-called Plodsbury Manuscript, believed to be in Chaucer's own hand and preserved in the Town Hall there on the right. It adds the following lines to the General Prologue:

An oother pilgrim there should have come doon
From Plodsbury, which is ycalled a very nice toon
But he did oversleep hem in his bedde
And so to Caunterbury he took the train instedde.

Some scholars have cast doubt on the authenticity of this fourteenth century document, but I suspect they are motivated by professional jealousy. Their assertion that Chaucer's words appear to be written on the back of a Chinese takeaway menu should likewise be disregarded.

On your left now you can see Plodsbury's premier tourist attraction, the Museum of Toothpicks. This is believed to be the largest collection of toothpicks in the western hemisphere, and attracts up to seven visitors annually. Next door to that is 35 Dullington Road, once home to Plodsbury's most infamous citizen: Haigh the Trouser Press Murderer. Taking inspiration from the only-slightly-more-famous Haigh the Acid Bath Murderer, Malcolm Haigh intended to dispose of his victims by compressing the bodies into nothing by means of a Corby trouser press. Haigh's reign of terror was brought to an end before he actually managed to kill anyone by virtue of his being arrested, prosecuted and imprisoned for six weeks for the theft of a Corby trouser press, but I am prepared to speculate that his victims could have numbered into the hundreds.

Moving on, we come to the Plodsbury Asda. This is not in itself historically significant, except insofar as it is a perfectly preserved example of a mid-1990s supermarket. It is, however, built on the former site of Plodsbury Hall, the ancestral home of the wealthy Bibblewhipp family whose members have played an often-influential role throughout British history. For example, I'm sure you have heard of the time Sir Walter Raleigh laid his cloak in a puddle to allow Elizabeth I to pass without wetting her shoes; less well known is the fact that the puddle was caused by Sir Horace Bibblewhipp and his famous incontinence.

Sadly, Plodsbury Hall burned down in a tragic accident in 1987 when the late Sir Ethelred Bibblewhipp attempted to chase off a Labour Party canvasser by the application of a live hand grenade. You will be pleased to know, however, that although the Hall is gone, the Bibblewhipp family continues to go from strength to strength: the current head, Sir Agamemnon, is famed throughout the world for his peerless collection of stamps, coins and assorted memorabilia of the Third Reich. He currently resides at Her Majesty's pleasure.

Turning the corner here, we find ourselves on the banks of the River Ick. Local folklore says that the rocks by the side of the Ick can sometimes be seen to glow at night: some people say this is fairy fire, marking the Ick as the river down which King Arthur's funeral boat sailed as it took his body to the mystical island of Avalon, while others attribute it to the run-off from the nuclear power plant.

On the north shore of the Ick you can see our most famous statute, the Venus de Williams. Modelled on the Venus de Milo housed in the Louvre in Paris, this statue has tennis rackets for arms and was constructed by Plodsbury Primary School to commemorate the time that Venus Williams, the Wimbledon champion, once passed through the town on a bus.

Also by the riverside you can see the former house of the noted Victorian engineer, Isambard Kingdom Jones, so named by his father in the hope that he might match the greatest engineer of the Industrial Age. Alas Jones's absolute sincerity of purpose was known, on occasion, to founder on his utter lack of talent and engineering prowess. Due to a regrettable tendency to confuse feet and inches, his great masterpiece, the Plodsbury Grand Suspension Bridge, can be seen over the duck pond on the old village green.

Finally on the river, you can see the landing jetty for the weekly Plodsbury to Dunkirk ferry, which has run since 1976 aboard the SS Aarrgh Glug Glug, so named due to an unfortunate accident that befell the Princess Royal at the launching ceremony.

Turning left here, we now find ourselves on Short Street. This is in fact the longest street in the town, and excellently showcases the famous Plodsbury sense of humour. On the right here is the house of Plodsbury's most famous living resident, Jennifer Smith. Mrs Smith is the sister of that actress in *Coronation Street* – you know the one, that woman who had the affair, killed the bloke with the eyebrows and then ran off. I can't remember her name off the top of my head. Anyway, Mrs Smith is not herself involved in acting, but is sometimes at a distance mistaken for her sister despite being fifteen years older and only having the one leg. She is available for children's parties, weddings and bar mitzvahs.

And now we come to the glorious finale of our tour, the main town square. You may be wondering why this contains large-scale models of the Palace of Westminster and St Paul's Cathedral. These are a testament to the vital role played by Plodsbury in the Second World War. They were constructed by the Ministry of War as part of Operation Acceptable Losses. While the rest of the country was plunged into the blackout, at Churchill's personal order Plodsbury was in an enforced state of 'lights-up', with the hope that the Luftwaffe would mistake Plodsbury for London. Luckily for us, the Nazis were aware of the scheme, Goebbels himself sending the Prime Minister a personal note stating that the German propaganda machine would under no circumstances wish to deprive the English of Plodsbury.

Well, sir, that marks the end of the tour, which I hope you've enjoyed. Copies of my latest book, *Cultural Beacons of Europe: Rome, Vienna, Plodsbury*, are available for purchase in that bookshop there for only £39.99. We hope to see you in Plodsbury again soon, and may I take this opportunity to remind you that there are no refunds.

Tonia Bevins

SWEET WILLIAM

Lately I am haunted by a man
who looks at me then vanishes from view
as with a ship that slipping our horizon,
passes into blue. Or dew that steams
from grass as death unmists a looking-glass;
on silent feet a cat who comes at night
in sable coat, white pickadill at throat.

My phantom wears a ring of gold – a glint
that draws the eye to eyes that burn. And yet
his touch and breath felt cold upon my skin –
we cupped a flaring match against the wind.
I watched him alighting from the ferry boat
then lost him on the teeming bridge of Avon.

Have you seen Sweet William?

In the Chandos Portrait, WS wears a single earring.

Joyce Ireland

EPITAPH

Here lies Grace Smith
who has died.
She was the wife of Robert
who loved her.
The mother of Sarah
and grandmother to Jason and Jodie.
Her sisters, Vera and Enid, will miss her.
Her friends were Mary and Flo
and she once worked for Phyllis.
But, who was Grace?

Joan Dowling

THE GARDENER

She waits until he goes into his beloved garden, his favourite place when not beside her, then follows him.

Rising from the flower bed, he comes to meet her, love luminous in his eyes. She kisses him, then breaks his heart.

'I'm sorry,' she says. 'There's someone else. I have to leave you.'

His pain strikes her like a blow.

She weeps when he begs her to stay, but still turns away.

The garden is quiet after she's gone. As his tears fall on the last begonia, he pushes its roots deep into the ground, tenderly patting the earth around it.

He whispers. 'Until death us do part, my love.'

Bob Barker

THE STATUE

Across the river, the blood-orange sun was rising over the desert as the dhow eased into its berth next to the quay. On the deck, the crew bustled about, securing ropes, loosening stays, gathering in the great canvas sails, their job done until the next voyage.

Waiting at the end of the dock, Abu-Hotep pulled the edges of his linen jerkin together to ward off the chill morning air. Abu hated early mornings. If he had his way, he would not stir until the sun had warmed the air enough that he could bathe without shivering. But Abu's fondness for warmth wasn't the only reason that, right now, he was wishing the sun were higher in the sky. It would mean that the meeting with the man soon to disembark and which he had been dreading for the past two months, would be over and he would know his fate.

As Abu swept his gaze over the boat's length, he had no difficulty spotting the man he was seeking. Huge in stature compared to most men, Kalal-Hitam was standing at the vessel's stern. He was shaking hands and touching heads with a stocky Arab whom Abu took to be the captain. No doubt thanking him for returning him, safely, to his home port. *Praise Be To Osiris.*

Even as Abu saw him, Kalal-Hitam turned and, spotting his young pupil, raised an arm in greeting. Abu forced a smile and returned the gesture. Towards the bow, two bare-chested crewmen were already securing the gangplank to the quay. Turning, Abu made his way towards it. But by the time he got there, the great man was already striding down it.

'Greetings Abu-Hotep,' Kalal called as he stepped onto the landing stage, 'How is my most earnest pupil?'

'Greetings, Kalal-Hitam,' Abu replied, bowing to honour his Master as protocol dictated he must before speaking further. 'We thank the Great God Isis for your safe return and rejoice at your being amongst us once more.'

'It is good to be back, Abu,' the older man said, draping a large arm around Abu's shoulders and turning him so they could walk back along the dock to the waiting transport. 'And how are you? You look a little tired. Not used to these early mornings, I fear?'

Abu forced another smile. 'No, Master. I prefer rising when the Sun God has banished the night spirits and a man can see to his duties without having to wrap himself like a woman.'

Throwing his head back, Kalal laughed, heartily, and slapped the boy between the shoulder blades.

'But this is the best part of the day, Abu. Fresh, clean and free from the foul stench of camel dung.' As he finished, he made a point of breathing in deeply, then let it out with a long, 'Aaaaahhhhh.'

At that moment, the last thing on Abu's mind was the quality of the morning air, though he had to admit, there was a sweetness to it that would not be there in another hour or so.

'So tell me, Abu,' Kalal enquired as they stepped onto the firm ground of the river bank. 'How goes the work? Progress is good I trust?'

Abu hesitated. What to say? How could he tell him? The crowd was dense around the dock. He dare not reveal the news here. So many people should not witness his shame, though he was certain it was no more than he deserved. Choosing his words carefully, he replied, 'Much has been done, Master. The masons have worked long and hard.'

Familiar with his protégé's verbal nuances, Kalal threw him a glance. But Abu turned away, not yet ready to meet this master's gaze.

'Are these your bags, Master?' he said.

As they rode the cart towards the work-site, Abu felt his stomach churn as he sought the courage he needed to reveal how he had failed the man who had placed so much trust in him. And Abu knew that when he did, it would mark the end not just of his apprenticeship as engineer and master builder, but the end of his dreams of one day being the most famous builder in all of Egypt. Banishment would soon follow, if not worse. He may even end up a slave himself.

As they neared the site, the dust thrown up by the labours of the vast workforce rose in the air ahead of them. Abu saw his master lean forward, peering into the haze, excited at the prospect of seeing for himself how work had progressed during his six-month absence.

Privately, Abu had always feared that the absence of the Chief Architect for such a prolonged period may cause problems. But Kalal had been insistent. Pharaoh had demanded his presence at the building of the tombs in the north, and he had had no option but to comply.

'You will be fine, Abu,' Kalal had said as the day of his departure had drawn near. 'The masons have their plans and the labour has been secured. All you need do is monitor progress and report any problems to the overseer. I have seen you work and I know you can handle it. I trust you Abu. You will be a great builder one day. Greater even perhaps than myself.'

As he reflected on how he had betrayed his master's trust, Abu shook his head. Even now, he had trouble fully comprehending just how things could have gone so disastrously wrong.

Of course, Abu knew once the building work began following Kalal's departure, things passed out of his control quickly. It was almost inevitable. As only an 'in-locum' architect, Abu had little say in the work. Even when he raised his initial concerns, his queries were swept aside by the arrogant Master Masons.

Now, with hindsight, he could see it was a mistake to put another team of masons to work on the project. Something was bound to go wrong. But it was Prince Akham-Tut himself who had insisted. It was his decision that the first stage of the work should be completed sooner than planned and in time for his father's return from the North.

Abu recalled how he had urged the young prince to let him

travel to the north to consult with Kalal-Hitam, and even Pharaoh himself. But he would have none of it.

'We do not need their advice,' the prince had said. 'We know what to do. Leave the old men to their tombs and their caves. We will show them what we can do and when they get back they will be amazed by our enterprise.'

'What a mistake,' Abu thought to himself.

'What mistake?' Kalal-Hitam said.

Abu froze. So wrapped in his thoughts was he, he had not realised he was actually translating them into words.

'What mistake?' Kalal repeated.

Out of ideas and lying being against his nature, Abu knew he had no choice but to confess. He let out a sigh. Besides, they would be at the site within minutes. His master would know soon enough anyway. Throwing himself at his master's feet in the back of the cart, Abu began to wail.

'Oh great Master! Kalal-Hitam, Master builder and Chief Architect of all Egypt, I, your unworthy servant and Godforsaken pupil have dishonoured your great name and your great work.'

Shocked at his pupil's sudden show of remorse and piety but not yet knowing the reason for it, Kalal-Hitam looked down in astonishment at the youth now bowing and worshipping at his feet.

'Abu-Hotep,' he cried. 'What is it? Why do you prostrate yourself like this before your Master? What has happened?'

'Have no fear, Master,' the distraught youth continued. 'I will take full responsibility. I will leave Egypt forever and tell all that the great name of Kalal-Hitam should remain unsullied. That his ignorant, incompetent, assistant, Abu-Hotep was to blame and must for the rest of his life atone for his failure.'

Kalal-Hitam looked embarrassed. 'Get up, Abu,' he said. 'Everyone is looking. For goodness sake stop bowing and scraping and tell me what has happened.'

Sheepishly, tears flowing freely now, Abu took his seat again, though still unable to look his master in the face.

'You will see in one moment, Master. Oh what a disaster.

Such shame.'

Worry now etched across his face, Kalal-Hitam turned towards the site now coming into view. He peered forward straining to see what it was that had resulted in such a show of penitence and anguish from his lead apprentice. What sort of disaster could possibly have befallen this, his most prized project, without word of it reaching his ears before now? Bit by bit, the shape of the structure ahead began to emerge through the dust and the heat haze thrown up by the already hot sun. He turned to look back to his pupil, still hanging his head in shame, not yet able to bring himself to speak. Suddenly, the statue came fully into view and Kalal-Hitam gasped as he finally realised the cause of his pupil's anguish. The huge head looked out across the desert, the face unmistakable now in the morning sun.

'What?' he gasped. 'But how …?' Then he lapsed into silence, for the moment unable to comprehend what he was seeing.

Abu took a deep breath. It was time to explain. And as they rode closer to the immense structure, with Kalal-Hitam sitting next to him, struck dumb by the shock of what he was seeing, Abu recounted the sorry tale. Voice shaking, he told of how the young Prince had had the idea that they could surprise his father and finish the project early if he put another team of masons on it. How the Master Masons in charge of the two teams had conferred amongst themselves but had chosen to cut the young Architect out of their meetings. 'You are not the real Architect,' they said. 'You are merely an observer. Kalal-Hitam is not here. We are in charge. You go and count your labourers. We are the experts and we do not need a young upstart apprentice to tell us what needs doing.' Then they took the plans and split them between them. But something had gone wrong. Abu had tried to tell them, but they had ignored him and told him they knew what they were doing. Eventually they had barred him from the site so intrusive did they find his protestations and questioning of their work. And so the work had been allowed to progress for months without a resident architect, and with two teams of masons working at either end of the structure.

Perhaps if they had not been so keen to compete with each other, to hide their work from each other's view by screening their labours with sheets and canvasses then the mistake would have been realised before it was too late. But it had not and now ... Well, Kalal-Hitam could see for himself.

The cart stopped at the base and they climbed out. Kalal-Hitam still said nothing but simply stared up at the structure and along its great length. Of course, it was not yet finished. Nowhere near. It would be many years before work on it would end, or so it had been planned.

In fact, Kalal-Hitam was amazed at just how much work, of a sort, had been completed. The outline was clear, and the form of the head and body were unmistakable. Far too late to change now, he reflected. Kalal saw at once how it had happened. As soon as Abu mentioned another team of masons and described their arrogant assumptions that they knew what they were doing, he had grown worried. He knew masons. As craftsmen, they were good at their job. But they always need guidance. Without an architect present to interpret the plans, they are always liable to make mistakes.

And this was a beauty.

He could imagine how the mix up had occurred. He could see it in his mind. He knew now he should have ensured that all the sets of the previous plans – his initial proposal – were destroyed, or at least stored away, far from the site. Then such a mistake could not have occurred. But there was no way he could have known that another team of masons would be put on the project during his absence, or that they would have started working to the wrong set of plans.

When he had gone away he had anticipated that by the time he returned, the work would still only be a rough outline, plenty of time to correct any slight mistakes. But now, with two teams of masons, it had progressed too far to go back. It was too late to re-shape it.

Kalal-Hitam stood with hands on hips looking at the

stonework. Abu-Hotep stood next to him wringing his hands, waiting for the reaction. What was his master thinking? When would he turn on him and begin to berate him for allowing this, the greatest project in all of Egypt's history, to go so badly wrong?

'The plans for my initial proposal,' Kalal-Hitam said evenly, placing a heavy hand on Abu's shoulder.

'Master?' Abu-Hotep said, unsure what he had meant.

'The new team of masons you mentioned. They took the plans for the initial proposal.'

Abu nodded, his eyes cast downwards to the sand. 'A calamitous mistake, Master. I did not realise until too late. They would not let me interfere. I tried to tell them.'

Kalal-Hitam nodded. He had actually been quite proud of his initial proposal. He had liked the idea of a representation of Pharaoh himself sitting there at the entrance to the city looking out over the desert.

But the court and Pharaoh himself had rejected it and had called for something more symbolic, less personal. Something that reflected Egypt's heart and strength. That was when the idea came to him. A form that would represent Egypt's place in the world, how the Land Of The Pharaohs was the dominant force in the world of men. And Pharaoh had liked the idea. Approved it. Ordered that the statue, as proposed, be built outside the city, next to the great pyramid. A statue that would stand there forever; an ever-lasting symbol to the power and majesty of ancient Egypt.

Abu stood there, hanging his head in shame, feeling his master's hand still resting on his shoulder. He could feel him quivering with anger. The storm was about to burst. Daring a quick glance, he lifted his gaze, and was amazed by what he saw. Instead of blood-red rage, his master's face was creased in a smile. He was actually chuckling to himself, his large frame shaking with laughter.

'M...Master?' he enquired. He has taken leave of his senses, he thought. The shock has turned his mind. But as Kalal-Hitam turned to look down on him, he seemed in full possession of his faculties.

'Have no fear, young apprentice. I know this is not your fault. You will not be banished. Nor sold as a slave.'

'But ... But what about Pharaoh? Will he not want to have us both killed, or worse, for what has happened to his great project?'

Kalal-Hitam looked up at the structure above them. 'It is too late to do anything now. The work has gone too far. But maybe all is not lost. There is a symbolism here, an unintended one maybe, but a symbolism nevertheless.'

Abu looked at his master now stroking his chin in amazement. He looked up, then back to his master again.

'You think ... you think ...?'

But His master interrupted him, draping his arm around the young man's shoulders. 'The great Pharoah portrayed for all time as having the head of a man, and the body of a lion? You know Abu, I think I might just be able to get him to go for it.'

Then, throwing his great head back, Kalal-Hitam let out a deep booming laugh, that grew in volume and caused everyone, masters, slaves, overseers, craftsmen, to scratch their heads in wonderment as to what, in Osiris's name, could be so funny?

Joyce Ireland

FRISSON

We are on a day trip to Venice, our first visit to this lovely city on the water. As we have arrived reasonably early, it isn't too crowded; we are fortunate that the queue for St Marks is fairly short and we join it.

This beautiful eleventh-century Byzantine cathedral is awe-inspiring, with magnificent tiles decorating its interior. We decide to go up to the upper gallery where one can see the original bronzes of the four horses of the Apocalypse which once stood outside over the entrance. They have been replaced by replicas and housed for their protection from the effects of the weather in an L-shaped room.

As we marvel at these amazing sculptures, my companion moves out of sight round the corner and for a few moments I am completely alone with the huge beasts. It is very quiet and I am very aware of the sensation of movement that the sculptor has achieved. I feel very privileged for this private viewing of such a noble group of animals. I stand and gaze at them as they appear to rear up and toss their manes proudly. I don't want this moment to end.

Then others enter the room and the spell is broken.

Mark Acton

BONE

Bone! Bone! Give me the bone! Come on, give me the bone, quickly!

Mmm, bone. I got it. I got the bone. Check me out. I got a bone. I got a bo-one. It's in my mouth A tasty bone.

Drop it on the floor. Stare at it.

Ooh, a bone! On the floor! I want that bone. What if someone gets the bone before me? No one better get that bone. I want the bone. I'm gonna stalk that bone. I'm going to prowl around it, nose to the ground, bum in the air. Stay there, bone! Don't you go running off with anyone else. Just stay there and be a good bone. I've got my eye on you. I'm ready. One false move and I'll pounce. That's it. Good bone.

No. I don't trust you. I'm going to pick you up in my mouth and fling you across the floor.

Yeah, like that.

Now, where've you gone?

There you are. Were you trying to hide from me? Bad bone. Come here. I've got my eye on you. I don't trust you. Come here.

Mmm, bone. I got a bone. It's in my mouth. Big tasty bone. And it's all mine. You can't have it. It's my bone.

I'm going to hide it. Somewhere you'll never find it. Got to find a good hiding place. Let's try the kitchen. Nah, no good in here. How about the hall? Nope. What about upstairs.

Why am I up here? I need to get downstairs to my family. They've all left me on my own up here. I bet they're gone forever. I'm going down with my bone.

Oh hi, everyone. I got a bone. In my mouth. A big tasty bone. You can't have it. It's mine. I need to bury it, so you can never find it. How about behind this cushion? Don't look. Oh no, the cushion's fallen on the floor. I'm never going to find anywhere to hide it now. What am I going to do? Help. Ooh, how about *this* cushion? Oh yeah, that's good. Just move your bum so I can get behind here. That's it. Just shift along. Come on, I've got important work to do here. That's it.

Oh yeah, check me out. I hid my bone. No one can find that now. I am the champion of all bone-hiders in the whole world!

Mmm, I smell bone. That smells good. Someone's hidden a bone in here. Now, where's that bone? I'm gonna find that bone. I can smell you, where are you?

Oh yeah, it's coming from behind your bum. Come on, shift it. Move that butt, I've got important work to do here. That's it. I'll just knock that cushion on the floor and there she is...look at that beauty!

I got a bone! Check me out. I'm the champion of all bone-finders in the whole world. And it's my bone. It's so good to have you back.

Shantele Janes

THE MAN WHO TRAVELLED WITHOUT CLOTHES

His bare bottom bobbed
like two apples past their sell-by date,
shrivelled, brown and soft
against the sweat-stained leather seat.

Mouths gaped as he passed,
a flesh-coloured streak on wheels.
Old ladies dropped their shopping bags
in shock.
And women
with small children hurriedly
covered innocent eyes.

Others stifled sniggering,
while blue-haired pensioners on discount day
stepped outside to see,
and adjusted their spectacles
'just to be sure'
whether he was indeed nude.

But the man who travelled without clothes did not mind.

They commented on the awkwardness of his shape,
his pointy knees
that jutted like splintered bone from the frame,
drawing the eye downwards
towards whirring pedals
and his only confinement –
pulled high on the calf –
white towelling socks,
poking through worn leather sandals.

His liking for naked travel had started in youth,
when he had for the first time
experienced the fluttering
kiss of breeze
against his adolescent skin,
riding fast away from the taunts,
shirt billowing behind,
absorbed into a sunset,
that burned as brilliant
as his hair.

So he does not mind the stares,
the pointing, the muffled giggles
that greet him as he passes.
For he is unwrapped, naked, free.

Deborah K Mitchell

HIMMELWEG

Come closer Julia, for I have something I need to say to you.
But first, could you fetch me some water? And maybe open
the window a fraction, so the curtains billow in the breeze?
You know how I enjoy seeing the shafts of sunlight filter
through the lace.

Thank you, my love. That's better. Isn't it beautiful?
What more could a dying man wish for than to have his
beloved sit beside him with her long, cool fingers stroking his
forehead? And for a summer breeze to blow gently across his
skin? Perhaps you could play the piano downstairs for me later.
I can drift to sleep listening to your wonderful compositions.

I have loved you so much, dear Julia. I remember the first
time I saw you, playing Arabeske at the recital in Delft, where I
was teaching at the University. I knew then that this was the
woman I wanted to spend the rest of my days with. You have
made me a very happy man. You, Ari and Saul. I never thought
I could be so happy.

But there is a secret I keep within me, Julia. I hope in its
telling, you will know me better, and see what lies at the centre
of my soul. This dark spot, which I never revealed to you. I
must reveal it now. I cannot take this with me to the grave.

It was 1942. I was a barber by trade, back then. Yes, I know
this must be a surprise to you. I had many loyal customers at
my little shop in Częstochowa, the town of my birth. The
business thrived. I was good at my job. But everything changed
that freezing cold winter.

I remember, the snow lay thick on the ground that year. It
was the type of cold that crept beneath your skin and found its
way right into your bones. That was the winter when my
family, friends, neighbours, and I were transported by train
from the ghetto, to the camp at Treblinka.

It was a place we had never heard of, and we thought it strange that the Germans told us we were going there to work. Why would children and the elderly be crammed onto the same train as those of us being sent to labour? We could not question the guards, of course. We had no choice but to believe what they said.

It soon became clear though, when we arrived at Treblinka – trembling with cold and hunger and thirst and fear – that only a very few of us were needed for work. Those of us who had certain skills, which the Germans could make use of. Who would have thought that my talent with a comb and a pair of scissors would be my salvation? If that's what you could call it.

My darling, I hesitate to tell you this and I am deeply sorry that I kept this from you all this time, but I was married before you.

Oh, I am sorry to upset you. Here, let me kiss your hand. It is a shock, I know.

Her name was Arielle. She was just 19 years of age when we married, and I was 20. Just a year later, we welcomed a daughter into our little family. Yes, my love, I had another child. It was all such a long time ago now. Please, Julia, remember that this was another life. I was a different person then.

My daughter's name? We called her Talia. Our beautiful Talia.

When we disembarked from the train at Treblinka, I was separated from Arielle and Talia. All of the men were separated from their wives and daughters and sisters and mothers. Only the old stayed together. The old, who were told they were going to the camp's Infirmary to be cared for. The Infirmary which turned out to be a pit, where their naked bodies were thrown and burned. I remember the smoke from the pit. And the stench of charred flesh.

A few weeks after my arrival, the Germans sent out an order for any barbers in the camp to come forward. There were seventeen of us. You may ask, why would they need barbers? In such a place, why the need to cut hair? Well, let me tell you the terrible reason why.

The guards took us to a place that was hidden, behind gates and trees and barbed wire. This was what they called *Himmelweg.* The Way to Heaven. The hidden place was a room. Quite small, maybe twelve or thirteen square feet, with wooden benches set about it. This was where the women and children came, stripped of their clothing and dignity, to have a shower. But you know, of course, that this was no shower room.

The guards told them they would have a haircut before they washed, to help keep them clean and tidy. Some of the women guessed what the real reason was for being there, and they screamed and pleaded. Such a harrowing, desperate sound. I still hear those screams, Julia.

So, we barbers were ordered to take the hair from these women and children. Hair that would be sent to the factories and turned into textiles and such like. Oh, but some of those tresses I cut off. Beautiful, long hair, just like yours. And the colours – chestnut and auburn, blonde and russet. The colours of sunny days and autumn leaves. We were given two minutes in which to chop away at their curls, their silky curtains of hair.

And when we were done, and the women and children were all shorn, the barbers were instructed to leave the room. We were made to stand outside for maybe twenty minutes or so, while the gas did its work, and then the cleaning detail mopped up the excrement that those poor souls left behind.

Then we went back inside and did it all over again, with another batch of women and children. More screaming and pleading and crying. More snipping and cutting and trying not to think about what we were doing. The lie we were telling.

There was nothing we barbers could do to save these wretched people. Any words of protest from us would have been met with a bullet in the head. The guards were ever watchful. They had given us a job to do. We had to do it.

You have no idea how sickening it was to tell a neighbour or friend from Częstochowa that I was going to make her look nice. To sit a naked woman down on a bench and lie to her, all along knowing that she would never see daylight again. It hurts my heart, Julia. It grips my insides like a fist of iron.

Yes, I would like another sip of water, thank you. And if you could close the window now, for I have grown cold. This is a lot to take in, my darling, I know. I will understand if you need a minute.

You want me to continue? Yes, of course.

As I said, that winter was so dreadfully cold and we waited outside that terrible room in our thin striped uniforms, shivering. We were silent. No one spoke. What was there to say, when we knew what was happening just a few feet from where we stood?

We returned to the room. More women. More frightened little children. More chopping. More waiting outside in the snow while all those lives slipped away.

And so it went on, until my mind became numb and my eyes and fingers were sore from the work and the cold. I was just going through the motions then. I had somehow managed to emotionally detach myself from it all. That changed when I heard someone call my name.

'Jacob,' she shouted. 'Jacob!'

I turned towards the sound and saw them. Thin, and pale and naked. My darling Arielle and our sweet, sweet little Talia.

My wife picked up our child, who was just five years old, and began to push her way through the crowd of women towards me. With tears in my eyes, I shook my head to tell her *no, you must stay where you are. The guards. They have guns.*

She must have understood, because she stopped and put Talia back down, and Tomasz, one of the other barbers, guided them to one of the wooden benches. In the crush of people, I managed, unseen by the guards, to make my way across the room to where my wife and daughter sat.

I cannot tell you what emotions churned within me, Julia. Well, you can only imagine. Knowing that the two people I loved most in the world were breathing their last breaths.

I had to swallow down bile, and tell my frantically beating heart to slow down, and I had to keep my hands from shaking as I gathered Arielle and Talia to me and hugged and kissed them and told them I loved them and I would see them again soon, in a better place. All the while trying to keep out of sight of the guards.

I had to keep the tears inside my eyes, as I ran my fingers one last time through their lovely hair. In just a few minutes, it was over. Arielle and Talia were taken from me. I remained at Treblinka for more than a year after that, until my escape. Every day I cut hair in that Hell, in a state of mental paralysis.

How could I do that? How could I go on living, after my wife and child had been slaughtered?

Well, how could any of us do it?

How could Josef the train driver, plied with vodka by the Germans, roll the locomotive and the packed cars into Treblinka station day after day, seeing the corpses of those who had suffocated or died from thirst during the journey? Sending his living passengers to their deaths.

Or Piotr and Aleksander, the Polish farmers whom I later befriended. How could they go to work in their fields, when smoke rose from pyres and the stench of death hung in the air like a poisonous fog?

I have asked myself this question, Julia, many, many times. I ask myself this question still, every day, as I lie here, propped up against the pillows like a wrinkled, ancient rag doll who will soon wither away to dust.

Was it self-preservation that made us obey the guards? Cowardice? Or a feeling that no matter what monstrous tasks these people presented us with, we would never be defeated. We would survive. We would not give our souls to them.

I struggle to comprehend the horror of it, and I struggle with the memory of it. Turmoil squirms in my guts like a restless demon. But the clock ticks now towards my day of reckoning.

I hope Julia, you can forgive me for this secret. I hope I was a good husband to you and showed you all the love I felt, and still feel, for you. Please tell Ari and Saul how much I love them too. You are everything to me.

But I have one last thing to show you now. I kept them

hidden within the pages of the Holy Book I have on my nightstand. Yes, I took them out when you went to fetch my water.

But now my fingers hurt from clasping on so tightly. Here, see.

This one, this russet-coloured curl, belonged to Arielle. The soft, blonde ringlet. That was my Talia's.

Let me keep them with me, my darling. My time, it is close now.

I beg of you, all my loves, to please forgive me. Goodnight Julia. Goodnight my darling.

Gwili Lewis

A WRITER'S PRAYER

May be sung to the hymn tune Blaenwern

Thank you Lord for love and blessings
And the gifts bestowed my way.
Guide me as I toil at writing
Prose and poetry every day.

CHORUS: You're the Word and its Creator,
Talent Giver so sublime.
You're the Alpha and Omega,
Be it thus till end of time.

All around me there is sadness,
Broken homes and endless strife,
May my words bring joy and gladness
And give hope for better life.

CHORUS: You're the Word and its Creator,
Talent Giver so sublime.
You're the Alpha and Omega,
Be it thus till end of time.

Thank you Lord for inspiration
As I daily wield my pen;
This, my prayer of adoration,
Glory be to Thee. Amen.

CHORUS: You're the Word and its Creator,
Talent Giver so sublime.
You're the Alpha and Omega,
Be it thus till end of time.

Liz Leech

THREADS OF TIME

Life is like a thread. It lengthens,
As a moonbeam vies with starlight
To create its own validation.

Weft thread glides through warp threads vistas
As the shuttle slides to release its burden.

Spun with care, the thread should not be broken
But repaired with a hasty weaver's knot,
Its blasted colours pattern the cloth
until the spools run empty

To leave behind a lasting treasure,
An imprint of emotion.

David H. Varley

THE WORLD UNMADE: FIVE PROSE POEMS

I. Prologue. Untune the Sky

I set off by car on my habitual journey north on a bright and cold March morning. It is a drive I do often, travelling from my family home to the university city where I live and work. I have long since grown bored with it.

I ran into traffic almost immediately, and lost an hour I could afford to discard but did not want to. I listened to old tunes on the old radio, and willed the hours and the miles to pass.

The weather was clear, even temperate. I drove beneath a sky of impossible size, cloudless and vast, distant and heartfelt. As I climbed into the Pennines along the M62 the weather closed in, a subtle suddenness. Rain and snow mingled, a wetness, and I was driving within arm's reach of the leaden clouds. Fearing the worsening of the weather, I pulled off the motorway into a lay-by, and sought to test the air and work my legs. I left the car, and entered the world.

I became conscious of shapes in the field beside me, an impression of people obscured by the falling snow and rain. Compelled by something I cannot name, I left the road to tread uneasily and clumsily through the mud towards them. A great multitude, men and women, stood in silence, unmoved by the weather.

'Who are you?' I asked.

One replied: 'We are the poets, and the painters, and the music makers.'

'What are you doing here?' I inquired further.

Another replied: 'The world is ending, and we come to mourn it, to witness it and to hold wake.'

I did not believe them. They were glum, and serious, and

impossibly distant. But am I not a poet? Have I not, by artistic impulse alone, moved to sorrow, to delight? As a poet, I claimed my place.

'May I join you?' I said. 'I am a poet.'

There was a sensation of movement, the passage of but a moment, as if the universe let slip a sigh. The figures remained unutterably still.

A third spoke: 'No.'

I had not earned my place amongst them, and there would be no reconsideration. I returned, cold and saturated, to my car and began to drive. And the radio talked of commerce, of sand, of champagne, and I knew the world had ended.

II. *Remembrance. The Land Beyond the Sea*

I remember clearly the morning I first saw the land beyond the sea.

For all the ages of man before that dawn, the sea had stretched out plain and unadorned to the uncaring horizon. As the sun rose, I saw a land there, a land where once there had been nothing. Forests and woods gave way to sheer mountainsides that rose to snow-capped peaks shining in the early sunlight. Distance is deceptive on the sea, but we are a fishing folk with salt in us, and not a man or woman in the village reckoned the land to be more than a dozen miles away. An intrepid few, the first, climbed into their skiffs and sailed for the land beyond the sea. We waited for them to return, but they did not. When the next dawn came, the land beyond the sea was still there, still the same, but our kin had not returned to us, nor ever would.

And some men began to whisper dark words and think dark thoughts. They said that the land beyond the sea was cursed, that it boded evil, and they averted their eyes that they might not have to look upon it. Yet those strange woods and mountains filled the entirety of their horizon, the entirety of their world, and so their world became one of fear and pain: no man can fish if he cannot look upon the sea.

Day by day and year by year we lived in fear, forever in the sight of the land beyond the sea. Then some began to say that it was wrong to be in such terror, that there was a paradise over the waves, and that the sons and husbands, daughters and wives who had gone hence had found their every pleasure met. And many of my folk, long oppressed by their fear of the land beyond the sea, whooped with joy and raced to the shoreline, launching their boats to sail across the intervening water that they might be reunited with their loved ones.

The days passed, and they did not return. Those who had spoken of the delights of the land beyond the sea were gone, as were those who were most fearful of it. Those of us that remained held council. One of the elders spoke of the land beyond the sea, and of the danger it posed to us all, for had it not already taken so many of our kin? Others spoke in agreement, saying that the undiscovered country was an enemy, that it would move against us, that it must be dealt with. I was silent.

War was declared, war upon the land beyond the sea. The soldiers who had lately been fishermen rushed to their craft, brandishing their harpoons and singing their new battle cries. They would make war upon the land beyond the sea, and free their kin from the bondage of paradise.

I, who alone remained, have not seen my people since.

III. Glass. Beneath a Frail Faith

As I stood at a crossroads, awaiting friends, an old man approached me and spoke.

'If you pass along this route of my existence, and tread the darkened cloisters of this little world, following the path of heart and grave until on bended knee you kneel before the slow, dissolving firmament, then there, stripped of reason and meaning, you will feel your humanity shudder within you, and quail before the terrible noise that lurks in the heart of silence.'

IV. Pulchritude. Erda Rises

The lights grow dim, the chatter fades as the auditorium descends into an expectant hush.

She appears on stage, radiant and beautiful under the spotlights. Her hair is the colour of blood, her eyes the reflection of my desire, her skin the soft blush of promise. She wears nothing but a simple shift of white silk that runs down the contours of her body like milk. She is barefoot upon the stage, the whole material universe beneath her.

It is not about lust, you understand. Nothing so degenerate, so developed: it is a sensation older and more primitive than even lust. A hand, a mouth, a welcoming cunt will see to the needs of the body. This, for me and for the audience, is to satisfy a spiritual need.

She speaks:

'To know me is to understand a feeling, and to feel an understanding. I am me, I am Freyja, I am Ēostre, I am Fortune, I am Mother Church, and I am. Men have genuflected before the bitch-goddess since before they understood themselves, holding their manhoods in their hands and praising me with every joyous stroke. And they have clicked their rosaries and hailed my virginity in their sacred spaces. Image upon image, light upon light, they are the same. I will show you the gateway. I will show you the consolation of loss, the perfect imperfection. I will show you the two-way passage of life. I will show you the beginning and the end of existence.'

She lifts her shift. Between the fullness of her thighs I see the centre of the world, the image of my god.

V. Impermanence. The Maggots in God's Flesh

The human condition is one of anticipation tempered by a sense of our own diminishment. We look forward, but in looking to the future our thought alights only on the end of things, the days on which we shall run out of oil, of trees, of air, of light.

What if creativity is a finite resource? The thought occurred unexpectedly to me, and I wondered whether it was insight or heresy. What if all creativity is but one invisible whole, slowly chipped away by every word of poetry, every note of music, every subtle brushstroke? Have I, in some way, used up this precious stock, even in the production of these few words?

I am the artist thwarted by my art. Not a great poet, perhaps not even a good one, and yet, selfishly, I draw upon the limited impulses of my species, a mediocre king staking out his fiefdom of questionable ambitions and cancerous appetites. It is a self-reflexive impulse: to question art in the form of art, a process of auto-cannibalisation that word by word and thought by thought creeps ever closer to an ending.

Because it will end. We artists feast upon that which both sustains and houses us, tearing at the heart of it. Our thoughts race down the route of our destruction, hastening our slow extinguishment with every passing heartbeat. When the stock of ideas is spent, and humanity languishes in the faded temples of some better age, we will know only the certainty of ending, we who in looking forward see only into nothing.

Joan Dowling

THE BEST MEDICINE

The hospital elevator delivers the group of sombre faces back down to the ground floor. I close my eyes to shut them all out. So, nothing fatal then. Just the unwelcome prospect of more visits like this one. I know I should be grateful, that the alternative to getting old is not being here at all. But the compensations are getting fewer and further apart. You have to dig deep to find any at all.

Suddenly I sense that I'm being watched. I open my eyes, look down and meet the intense gaze of a small child.

'I like your white hair!' she shouts.

We all laugh.

Carolyn O'Connell

REMEMBERING THE FARM

I remember a farm where grasses grew,
wild flowers scattered over their jewels,
enriching the meadows where cattle grazed
and every August with horses we made hay.

The land was productive and the cattle thrived
and gentle the rain that watered the soil.
The summers were long and the children swam
in the waves lapping beaches of silvered sand.

For the cattle provided pure milk by the gallon
that was milked every morning and collected
in churns. It tasted so sweet fresh from the udder.

The grasses provided sweet hay for both horse and cattle.
I remember the haymaking, pitching grass on the fork;
the haycocks rising their mounds on the fields
to dry in the long days of summer's sure sun.

But that was before the farms turned to spreading
chemicals promising ever-increasing production.
The flowers vanished together with the bees,
and the meadows no longer held cattle and horses,
for the cattle are housed in great lines of production

and their milk is pumped into vats for pasteurisation.
It's delivered in plastic that needs recycling or lands
in the sea we once swam in so freely but now is awash
with fish that are dying and fishermen's catches grow

ever smaller as the boats that caught mackerel no longer
tie up at the jetty we walked to on Sundays, to buy mackerel
for dinner. They're gone with the summer and the pure spring
water we drank by the bucket from the clear mountain stream.

Posted on 14th June, 2017 by The Bardo Group Beguines

Helena Abblett

I'VE BEEN HERE SINCE YESTERDAY

I've been here since yesterday,
and this morning I start to feel the darkness lift.
The orange sun peeks over the distant hills,
and I allow my mind to spread further across the fields.

First it reaches the old dry stone wall,
past the tea towel, damp with dew and stretched
over the pointed rocks.
Then it reaches the cows, chewing and mooing
patient greetings and gratitudes.

As my thoughts seep further
into the comforting return to nature,
they touch the trees at the foot of the hills,
and I finally begin to let go.

The picnic blanket beneath my feet
is a temporary cover for the mud and weeds.

The weight of the report I had to write,
the drain of the court case,
the prison of the housework,
and the mountain of ironing
that I never managed to conquer.

I draw my mind in,
and look into the tin coffee mug in my hands.
Arms cradled between my knees,
I count the bubbles gathered around the edge.

The rays are warming my face now.
The children will be up soon,
and families start to stir in nearby tents.
I hear the rasp of a zip as someone welcomes the day.

Let in the light and lightness,
for this is what's important.

Steven Capstick

A Collection of Flash Fiction

Ultimate Upgrade
Zeus had to sign off on the project. Laid out on the bench before him was the final prototype. In field trials, it had performed beyond expectations. The new configuration of limbs had given it a broad range of movement on land and in water. Its internal organs now meshed together perfectly and the development of five senses took its perceptive ability to a new level. But the real breakthrough had come when research assistant Clio introduced the method by which they would be able to perpetually install and update new software to their own brains. She called it reading.

The Reckoning
He stood amongst the crowd in the village square and as the official decree was made, his heart sank. Not only did the Emperor want money, he wanted everyone to make the great journey to pay tribute. They called it a journey but in reality it was a cull. The old, the sick and the very young would not make it across the desert. He had made it last time but that was without a heavily pregnant wife. He needed to think through what he should do next. Later, returning home, Joseph explained to Mary why he'd bought the donkey.

The Photograph
The photograph on the coffin shows a soft November sun breaking through and highlighting the dress by picking out stars and flowers in the lace. White carnations tumble from her hands in a waterfall bouquet. She smiles at the camera, her back to a studded, wooden church door. The headdress dominates the picture, flowing from her raven black hair down to her ankles. Soon after, I know her taciturn father turned to

his daughter and imparted the wisdom of the ages in words that stay with her for the rest of her life. 'Happy the bride the sun shines on.'

Destiny

The gold prospector's feet kicked up clouds of dust along the main street of Independence, Missouri. As they haggled, voices were raised, tempers frayed and punches were thrown. Frank was determined to be the first on the road west. He pushed to the front at the hardware store and silenced the protests with his fists. When he returned, Whisper, his native wife, had food stored in the wagon and a boy sat by her, to help on the long trek ahead. Billy was only a kid but he had put a bullet in Frank's back before the journey was over.

A Monopoly of Fear

Mayfair was no place for regrets. Boot had moved through Regent's Street and Bond Street aware of new houses and hotels everywhere. Top Hat was close behind. Should he say something, voice his doubts or bury them. He surprised himself when he said, 'I don't want to go to jail again'. Her answer was predictable, 'Don't be stupid, with all that money in the bank they won't miss it. Take a chance and roll the dice.' He held his breath, he had come a long way. The last thing he wanted was to go back to the Old Kent Road.

1989

He was the first agent to infiltrate the Stasi. It had taken years to get a British spy deep under cover but now he had gone quiet. Huge government resources had been deployed in East Germany, including MI6's elite 'Kingsmen' but to no avail. Moscow agent, 'Jack Horner' and Warsaw source 'Little Bo Peep' had heard nothing. The Secret Services were just going to have to accept that their prize asset had been shattered and putting it back together again could take years. It was hard to believe that the fall of the Berlin Wall had brought down Humpty Dumpty.

Les Green

PLAYTHING

This was the moment. She knew she couldn't put it off any longer. In a quick, hard, twisting action perfected over many years on obstinate jars of pickles and preserves, the bird died in her hands. It was surprisingly efficient – perhaps she was expecting some resistance? Or maybe she just wanted it to be something hard earned instead of something as easy as opening raspberry jam.

It seemed a good idea when it first came to mind. Of course that was before she knew anything about chickens, but these days she occasionally saw herself as Cheshire's answer to Felicity what's-her-name from *The Good Life*.

The dead bird was placed tenderly in the box with the four that had been killed outright by the cat. He was obviously better at this than she was, as those birds were barely marked; not a spot of blood anywhere and not a feather ruffled – but dead all the same. She seemed to remember hearing though that cats liked to play with their prey? Maybe she was wrong about that.

'Rest in peace Hazel, Dottie, Marilyn, Lena and Tandoori.' She said their names out loud. They all had names of course. She liked to name them as she thought it gave them an identity, but in all honesty the chickens never gave it a thought. The only thing on their mind was feeding time, and all the time was feeding time. Every blade of grass, every flower and every leaf were consumed like a plague of locusts had discovered the place. They all succumbed to ravenous beaks, and the garden had begun to look like the Somme when it rained, until Chloe finally decided that the concept of free range had to have a limit enforced. To the chickens this was another thing not to think about so they put it on their list between 'names' and 'cats'.

She carried the box back to the house, checking that the gate was properly closed behind her. The other chickens carried on as though nothing had changed, but there might be a little more food until Chloe remembered to adjust the amount she was ladling out.

The real problem was the cat of course. She'd seen him hanging around the place but he usually stayed well away from the house and had never actually stepped a stealthy, dangerous paw into the garden as far as she knew. Not until last night anyway. She looked up to the low wall where she had seen him sit on many previous occasions, not expecting to find him but there he was – imperious and dangerous. His staring amber eyes covered the yards of garden with the directness of a laser. Meeting Chloe's furious gaze without remorse, he blinked slowly, which Chloe read as self-congratulation, and then brought up a white-tipped paw which received a single lick before being put down again. He then poured himself off the wall like a can of black furry paint and disappeared.

Once he was gone Chloe turned her thoughts to the dead birds. What do you do with dead chickens? Asking Jack would be a mistake and would only start an argument – he would likely suggest a warming, restorative bath with carrots, onions and potatoes. Maybe last night she might have smiled at the suggestion but not today, definitely not today. So what are the options? Bury them in the garden I guess.

Chloe put the box of birds on the windowsill while she looked for the spade, then remembered that she'd brought it into the chicken run with her as she thought she'd be able to use it to dispatch the dying bird. She couldn't do it of course – it was too brutal. She looked up and could see the garishly painted handle almost throbbing yellow in the early morning sunshine. Leaning over the fence, she retrieved it and started to dig in a corner of the Somme that hadn't quite recovered yet. It didn't take long as the ground gave easily to the keen edge of the spade. In almost no time at all there was a hole big and deep enough to take the dead birds and the box. She dug a little deeper anyway – the last thing she wanted was for some other creature to dig them up. Dropping the box gently into the hole, she said their names again – this time in a whisper 'Rest in peace Hazel, Dottie, Marilyn, Lena and Tandoori'. It was funny at the time of course, but letting Jack name some of the birds seemed like a mistake now. Okay it wasn't a proper funeral, but if that cat comes back then she was going to find it difficult to mourn the passing of Kentucky, Nugget and Biryani. It was decided then; the surviving chickens would get proper names when she stopped for a tea break. Maybe names of flowers would be nice. How about Daisy, Violet and Rose? Perfect, it's done already.

Chloe gently sprinkled earth on the bodies until they were completely covered, then started dropping the remaining earth in by the spade load, finally tamping down the mound and then walking on it in her boots until it was as flat as she could get it.

She walked back to the house and sat on the bench to remove and clean her boots. She was almost all the way to the back door before she noticed the dead blackbird on the mat that covered the step. As she walked towards it, the differing shades of blackness of the feathers reflected in shades of iridescent blue and green, but by the time she'd bent to check, the colours seemed to fade and all that was left was the once beautiful body of another dead bird. Not a mark visible on it. No signs of violence or struggle. It was very light. It was so much lighter than a chicken. There was almost no weight in it at all. The bird's head flopped easily to one side as she put it into the trug that sat next to the door. She would bury it later but wanted to put it out of the way in case the cat came back.

Thinking of the cat again made her look to the garden wall. Chloe let out a gasp of surprise after realizing the wall was jam-packed with cats. Lots and lots of cats. It was difficult to count them as they writhed and repositioned themselves, with new cats jumping up to join them. So many colours and sizes.

One by one all the heads turned towards her – even those that were repositioning themselves or finding a place to squeeze in had focused on her, and they all had their thousand yard, emotionless stare switched to full. She chilled involuntarily as she realized something awful was happening. Chloe remembered again about cats playing with their prey and inched herself backwards towards the kitchen door, her hands trying to turn the knob behind her back while she tried her best to keep all of the cats in her sight. A couple dropped silently to the ground on the Chloe side of the wall and walked casually towards her. Others followed suit and landed softly to the ground, padding silently towards her. Chloe suddenly realized there were no wildlife noises. No bees buzzing about the flowers, no butterflies, gulls or pigeons passing over and no garden birds. The cats got within a couple of feet from her when the back door burst open and she fell into the house, landing on her back and banging her head on the cold quarry-tiled floor. She didn't feel the pain at that moment. She was more concerned with keeping the cats out. Still on her back, Chloe raised her knees halfway to her chest and kicked out with both feet – slamming the kitchen door closed as the first couple of cats landed silently on the kitchen windowsill. They were joined quickly by others, jostling for a place. Chloe stood up too quickly and it made her dizzy. She put out a hand and was steadying herself on the back of a kitchen chair when she noticed the cats leaping from the windowsill onto the flat roof of the extension. She stretched her neck a little more and saw them disappearing from the extension roof into the bedroom window. At the same time she began hearing them land on the bedroom floor. She hurled herself at the kitchen door, slamming it closed with a massive bang as a pack of cats padded down the stairs, keen to play with their new toy.

Tonia Bevins

ON SHAKESPEARE'S 450TH BIRTHDAY

You've shown us love gone bad, betrayal, madness:
we're your schemers, dreamers, driven creatures.

You speak to Everyman and for all time –
a realm that spans the gutter and the gods.

You'd feel at home in Liverpool this spring –
a reborn theatre staging one of yours.

Come back to weave the threads of soaps and sitcoms,
post your playwright's blog online each day,
go spinning through our virtual, wicked world.

Yes, we know all about your dodgy friends.
And we don't mind. We keep a few ourselves.

But tell us why she had to have at last
your second-best – a gift that still annoys –
and why your female roles were played by boys.

*Note: 'second-best' refers to the bed WS is said to have bequeathed
to his wife, Anne Hathaway*

Tom Ireland

SCHOOL DAYS ARE THE HAPPIEST

Linda Green was two years older than me. She was in the Alpha set. Of course she was. I wasn't. She had blonde hair and blue eyes and white skin and pearly white teeth. Athletic. Class monitor, teacher's pet. All the things I could never be. She dedicated all her spare time to me. To my destruction. Her nails scratched me, her fingers pulled my hair out, her hands stole my belongings and her tongue told lies about me. She and her gang waited for me after school every night. Then, that Monday night, I snapped back. Her mob waited, strung across the path, smiling. Fun time. I put my head down, made a fist of my right hand, and stuck my right arm out in front of me. Like a battering ram. Roman warships had battering rams. I charged like hell straight at her. I heard them laughing but I kept on. I hit her right in her mouth. I knocked three of those pearly white teeth right out. Blood was pouring from her mouth and from my hand but the pain was all hers. She stood, staring at me, too shocked to move. Her gang ran away, looking back at me, astonished.

She dropped to her knees, still silent. For some reason I tried to help her stand up, but she screamed. She went on screaming, scream after scream, till a couple of teachers turned up. I was weeping now.

'I'm sorry, Linda, I'm sorry. I didn't mean it.' I wasn't sorry, I was terrified. Oddly, nothing really happened to me. I was collected from the staff room by a couple of social workers and returned to the care home. I started at a new school the following Monday. A special school.

First published in Girl on Wheels, appears here with my full agreement.

Debbie Bennett

HUNT

He stood by the edge of the river, cupped his hands together and whistled.

Two people walking a dog on the other bank looked over at him curiously. A jogger glanced in his direction and an elderly couple sitting on the bench nearby frowned at him.

None of which was the reaction he'd been expecting. Where was Carl and what about the damned boat? He was already feeling conspicuous in a suit – his black shoes were caked in mud and the collar of the white shirt was bringing him up in a rash across his neck. There was still no sign of pursuit, but that didn't mean they weren't coming – they probably thought he was armed with more than the Stanley knife in his inside jacket pocket and were sensibly waiting for the ARVs to put in an appearance. No doubt they were watching from the windows, waiting to see where he'd go with the money.

Joe whistled again, feeling a twinge of panic. It wasn't supposed to happen like this. There were no cameras around here – this part of the river where the jetty was crumbling dangerously, was on the other side of the High Street, a row of shops and a service road away from the CCTVs of the town centre. Carl and Gaz had checked the place out, found the rear door of the newsagents, wedged the gate on the back yard and carefully planned his escape route from the security men filling the cash machine inside. Gaz was watching the front door of the shop and Carl was supposed to be on the boat just upriver – a quick getaway where the ARVs couldn't follow.

'They won't suspect you in a suit,' Gaz had told him. 'And you look far too angelic to be dangerous.' He'd scowled at that – looking twelve when you were nearly sixteen was not an advantage as far as he was concerned. Over the past few years, the lads at school had stuffed his head down the bog on numerous occasions, set his hair on fire more than once and pierced his ear with a rusty nail in a particularly painful incident. But pain had made him stronger – he'd broken the bully's arm and from that point onwards, violence had earned him acceptance in the gang. Joe wondered what his mum would say if she could see him now, but he hadn't heard from her in more than nine months since she'd married the jerk she'd run off with two years ago.

The elderly couple stood up, watching him anxiously. He glanced down and noticed the blood on his trousers for the first time. Shit. Where the fuck was Carl? He whistled through his hands a third time, looking up and down the footpath along the river and wondering desperately if there was escape in either direction. In the distance he could hear the faint wail of sirens.

'Three times and I answer.'

'What?' Joe spun around and nearly slipped over in the mud as he stepped backwards and away from the figure standing up close.

He was tall. Well over six foot, Joe estimated, and dressed in black leather trousers with some kind of tribal arty-farty tunic in swirling reds and yellows that made him look like he'd stepped out of some nutty reality TV show. Either that or he was a tree-hugger from some hippy-bastard knit-your-own-sandals commune. Joe didn't much care – he just wanted to get away before the filth turned up.

Joe turned away, but the man was in front of him again, regarding him coolly, measuring him. Something in his eyes made Joe think he wasn't entirely sane.

'Three times,' he repeated. 'And I answer.'

He really was a nutter. Joe whipped the Stanley knife from his pocket and thumbed the blade out. There was blood crusted along the edge. But the man didn't change expression. He took two paces back, reached behind him and over his shoulder and before Joe realised what was happening, there was a four-foot long sword pointed at his chest.

'That is a blade, boy.'

Joe dropped the knife in surprise. He looked over to the bench, but the elderly couple had sat down again. A young woman with a toddler in a buggy strolled past but didn't appear to notice either Joe or the stranger. The sirens had gone, along with the sound of traffic from the High Street and the birds from the park opposite.

'You are no longer of this world, boy. You are mine until you give me what I seek.'

Joe held out the bag mutely. There was at least two grand in there – probably more – but he wasn't going to argue with a sword.

'What is this? Do not play games with me, boy.' The man grabbed the bag with one hand and tossed it aside. Joe couldn't help watching as a wad of notes escaped and landed in the mud with a wet thunk.

'OK, mate. Whatever. You win.' Joe'd had enough. Carl and Gaz had dumped him, the cops would be here anytime soon and he couldn't afford to get caught with blood on him. There'd be no way he'd get bail, not with the Council about to repossess the house and dad just started a ten-year stretch in Wandsworth.

'You draw Beltain blood and make the Call. I answer. I cannot leave without the Quarry.'

'What the fuck are you on about, mister? Just take the fucking money.'

The sword tip pricked his shirt and sliced flesh. Joe kept very still. There was no pain but a small scarlet flower blossomed on his shirt. The stranger's mad eyes stared straight into his own and Joe felt his bladder release. Around him the air was chill, patterns moved impossibly on the man's tunic and this wasn't real, couldn't be real—

He opened his eyes, although he knew he hadn't been asleep. The sword was no longer aimed at his heart, but the man hadn't yet sheathed it. His tunic was still alive, crawling with colours Joe had never seen before; he tried to look away but realised there was nothing else – the river, the people, even the bag of money had vanished into soft white mist.

'Only the Queen may release me and she is not yet reborn.'

'The Queen. Right,' Joe squeaked in terror. 'Who are you?'

'I am Fionn.' The man seemed surprised at this. 'You are the Hunter and I am the Hunt. Now name the Quarry and let us begin – the Hounds grow impatient.'

'But I'm—'

'Name the Quarry!' Fionn roared and he seemed taller still, outlined in fire against the mist. Fine features melted and for a second Joe could have sworn there were antlers growing from his head. Then he seemed to fold in upon himself and he was man again, sheathing the sword and glancing behind, almost nervously.

Joe could hear baying dogs beyond the fog. He suspected that the minute he turned and tried to run, his status might change from the Hunter – whatever that was – to the hunted and it didn't sound like the dogs had been fed recently. His legs were like jelly anyway; he was wet and cold and his chest was stinging from the cut.

'I cannot hold them much longer, boy.' The man's voice was softer now. 'You must choose the Quarry or pay the price. The Hounds will feast.'

He found his voice again and managed to get it under control. 'You have to hunt whoever I choose?'

'That is the way of things.'

The dogs were closer. Joe fancied he could see red eyes all around him in the mists, soft pants, the occasional yelp. So who did he hate enough to send a pack of dogs after? His mum, for turning a blind eye as her boyfriend got the bedrooms mixed up night after night? His dad, for being too pissed to care, or even notice when the bailiffs turned up?

'Choose, boy. I cannot save you if you do not name the Quarry!'

Hot breath on his legs. A nip on one ankle. And there were horses now, too, hooves thundering in from a distance, inhuman voices shrieking through the fog.

Out of nowhere, a black stallion appeared, foaming at the mouth and nostrils steaming. With a yell that made Joe want to piss himself again, Fionn leapt up on the creature's bare back. The horse reared, screaming with a voice that belonged to neither man not beast and the rider reached down, yanking Joe's arm so hard, he thought it must snap in two. And yet somehow he was astride the animal, clinging to the man's back as they were away into mist that was darkening by the second.

'The Hunt rides!' Fionn's cry wobbled on the edge of hysteria. Wild laughter answered back from the fog and Joe clung on for his life. Under his hands, flesh became fur, then feathers and he closed his eyes, wondering if he'd end up as insane as the rest of them. He could feel the Hounds streaming to either side, somehow keeping up with the impossible pace, although he knew that they were galloping beyond solid ground and that falling off now was not even an option.

And just as suddenly they stopped. The mist cleared and they appeared to be on a grassy hill in the middle of nowhere. It was dark, moonless, and the night sky was bright with stars. Joe half-fell from the horse and sprawled on the wet grass; looking up into hot dog-breath and red eyes, he scrabbled backwards in panic, coming up against the legs of another man, a second rider who hauled him to his feet.

If Fionn had scared Joe, then this creature was beyond terror – while he seemed human in appearance, there was nothing remotely human in his eyes. His form seemed solid enough when Joe looked at it directly, but the edges were constantly shifting, streaming away from his body like heat haze over tarmac. Even his clothing was changing subtly each time Joe looked – black leather became grey fur which shed itself to reveal an emptiness that made Joe's head hurt. His grip on Joe's shoulder was sending icy tendrils into his skin.

'Such sport, boy. Beltain blood is strong tonight.'

Fionn stepped in. 'He has chosen, my Lord. He is not for your pleasure.'

Joe looked around. The Hounds had fanned out and formed a ring around them – Fionn, this other rider and their mounts. Outside of the circle, other horses and riders prowled and paced impatiently. And he had chosen apparently, although he'd spoken nothing aloud.

The rider released him and waved a hand in the air. 'Your choice is in your heart, boy. It is obvious to those with eyes to see.' In the middle of the ring Joe saw Gaz appear, small and naked on the grass. His eyes were glassy and he was drooling.

Gaz. He'd always been the ringleader – the one with the hammer who'd nailed Joe's ear to the doorframe, the one who crapped before forcing Joe's head down the bog. It had always been Gaz from his first day at the comp, when they'd spat in his dinner and made him eat it—

Gaz, for the shit in his hair and the rusty earring – never mind what they'd done to him today.

Gaz – who was utterly defenceless in front of him.

'Where will you go?' he whispered to the rider, half-expecting to be blasted out of existence for daring to speak.

'To the ends of the earth and beyond.' The way he said it made Joe shiver. He inclined his head slightly. 'But you must speak the word. The Hunt requires it.'

'The – word?'

'The Hounds will have a soul this night. His or yours, it matters not to us.'

Joe looked at Fionn in desperation. To hate the pathetic whimpering youth in front of him was one thing, but to condemn him to this kind of Hell was another entirely. Gaz was muttering something, spittle leaking from his mouth and Joe realised he was still being chased by the Hounds, would continue to be chased beyond life and maybe beyond even death.

'And what if I change my mind?' Bolder now, he wondered how much power he actually held – after all he was the one who had spilled the blood. He was the Hunter.

Fionn drew a sharp intake of breath. 'It is not yet too late.'

'What if I choose one of you?'

The rider snorted. It was not a pleasant sound and Joe could feel his legs were about to give way. 'Do you think Danu's Riders burden themselves with souls, boy? That is a mortal affectation.' He smacked a riding whip against his gloved hand – or was it a claw? His image wouldn't keep still long enough for Joe's brain to catch up. 'I tire of this. Speak the word or the Hounds will feast twice this Beltain.'

The Hounds were moving in, snuffling and yelping, nipping each other in their haste. Beyond the pack, horses reared, wide-eyed and foaming while their dark shadowed riders let out the occasional howl; somewhere a horn blew long and low. Further out still in the shadows were lesser creatures, half-man half-animal and Joe couldn't tell where – or if – man ended and beast began.

And out on the very edge of the Hunt where the grass melted away into forever, there were humans. Or at least creatures that might once have been human, Joe was sure; the spectral glow that permeated the rider and the Hounds did not reach this far and he knew these were people, his own kind.

Danu's Riders have no souls, the rider had said. But what of those who followed the Hunt? Who were already living their own version of Hell following the Hounds across the sky?

Joe took a breath and willed himself to stay upright. Facing the rider he pointed beyond the Circle and out to the furthest reaches of the Hunt. 'I choose them,' he said, with more confidence than he felt. 'Any of them, take your pick.'

'You cannot—'

'I am the Hunter and I name the Quarry,' Joe interrupted. 'Them, out there.'

The Hounds backed away, turning in confusion. Horses stamped, voices muttered. The rider became a stag, pawed the ground and became the rider again. His aura blackened and Joe could feel an icy blast of air. The rider tipped his head back and howled at the night sky; Joe crouched down, his hands over his ears and wondered whether he'd ever see home again.

The sound abated. 'So be it,' the rider said softly and mounted his horse in a swift leap. He laughed loudly, cruelly, threw one arm in the air and looked back at the pack. 'We ride!' he shrieked as the horse jumped clear over Joe and the dogs, and galloped into the night, closely followed by the Hounds and the rest of the Hunt.

Gaz was gone too. Joe and Fionn stood alone on the hill with Fionn's mount.

'Boy, you are indeed the Hunter,' he said after a moment. 'Well met.' He swung up onto the beast. 'Travel your road in health, Hunter. I too must ride.' And he was gone, leaving wild laughter on the night breeze.

Joe watched a stream of light, a comet maybe, streak across the sky. It circled around, following the leader and hunting the follower in a bright spiral of stars that burned vividly into a pinpoint before dissolving into the streetlights of the town at the bottom of the hill.

First published in the British Fantasy Society's New Horizons in 2009

Bill Webster

MERLAK

Merlak shuffled backwards and urinated in the snow. He really didn't have any choice. He had to urinate, and there was snow blanketing the flat ground around him for as far as he could see in every direction. Trying to avoid urinating in the snow would have been a pointless exercise and would only have resulted in damp nether garments. Not a very bright idea in a sub-zero snow desert.

And in any case, sleeping within a circle of his own urine tainted with the devil weed he'd been consuming would greatly reduce the probability of his becoming a snack for one of the many feral creatures that appeared from their snow holes as night fell in these parts.

The devil weed was broken down by his metabolism and produced chemicals in his urine which were harmless and inoffensive to his species, but highly noxious to most of the creatures that prowled the Glatchian Snow Desert. It was an effective defence, and well worth the side effects.

It was the work of moments to throw up his sleep shelter and secure it against the sudden and unpredictable desert winds with guys and snow anchors.

Merlak turned, and noted how his metallic purple robes swirled and shimmered against the brilliant white snow. He smiled, and turned and swirled some more, marvelling at the interplay of colours and the associative images and tones released in his skull thanks to the psychotropic qualities of the devil weed. He floated a cam into position above his shelter and did some more swirls for art's sake. These pleased him greatly and he looked forward to sharing these images with his female... if he ever saw her again.

He sobered on the thought.

She was so beautiful, and they were very much in love.

They had been courting for many seasons now, and they had recently touched each other's foobahs. Merlak had found this most stimulating and pleasurable, and Liskae had shuddered and blushed. So they had done it again and Merlak had cammed the event for posterity, as was his wont.

His innocent mistake had been to post the evidence on Glatchinet, where Liskae's father had come across it (probably while searching for racy foobah footage) and had reported back to her mother. Once they had watched Merlak's camwork several times they consulted with Merlak's parents who came across for a viewing accompanied by social beverages and assorted pasties. There was much discussion and then the young couple were summoned.

Liskae assured them that Merlak had not pressured her and that she had actually quite enjoyed touching and being touched. The fathers gave each other knowing looks and then the grandfathers appeared inquiring if they might see the cam evidence too. And by the way, surely as elders they should be involved in such matters, and what had happened to respect for the wisdom of the older generation anyway?

Well, to cut a long story short, the grandmothers turned up next, and then the cousins and whatnot and before you could say 'Well fobble my foobah,' the whole fobbling village was there demanding to see the incriminating video evidence.

Merlak protested that it was not right that everyone should see his and Liskae's foobahs but was justifiably told that maybe he should have thought about that before he posted it on Glatchinet.

Several hours and many pasties and viewings later, the lovers' fathers went into a quick huddle and then Liskae's father addressed the gathering.

'Merlak and Liskae. Come forward and stand before me please.'

The young couple did as they were bid.

'It has long been the tradition of our people that foobah touching should not take place outside marriage. There are good reasons for this as the act of arousal triggers changes which cannot easily be accommodated outside a stable relationship. You both knew this and yet you gave in to your impulses.'

'But we are so in love, father and we do have...'

'Please. Be quiet, my daughter. I know of your feelings for Merlak, but you have broken our code and that cannot go unpunished. You are confined to your room immediately. Ladies, please escort her away.'

Led away by two of her grandmothers, Liskae hung plaintively onto Merlak's gaze for as long as she could.

Liskae's father turned to face Merlak. He sighed and shook his head.

'This gives me no pleasure, Merlak, but the code is clear. I take it that you do seek the hand of my daughter in marriage?'

'I most assuredly do, sir.'

'That is good, Merlak. That means you will live at least one more night.'

Merlak noted the unmistakable sound of a longsword being sheathed, and shuddered. This all seemed a lot more serious than seemed to be warranted by a little pleasurable foobah touching.

'Throughout these proceedings you have displayed disregard for the code. I understand that may be because you always intended to marry my daughter, so you thought it did not matter. But it does matter, Merlak. It is part of the glue that has held us together for centuries.

'I regrettably have no choice but to apply the provisions of the code, and perhaps now at last you will realise the seriousness of the situation and the peril you have placed my beautiful daughter in.

'Please bring the book, my wife.'

The large and ancient book was handed over reverently and there was absolute silence in the room except for the soft rustle of the dry pages being turned.

'Here we are. Section 6(b). Tests and Punishments. And at subsection 11... here's what we're after...'

He looked gravely at Merlak. 'Prepare yourself, boy. This

114

will be very hard for both of us.'

Was that a quiver Merlak detected in the man's voice?

'Insofar as it is written that a male will not touch a female foobah outside wedlock and that a female will not touch a male foobah outside wedlock, the following measures must be taken to discourage any recurrence in the wider population.

'The punishment for the female is death by being thrown from the top of Mount Herma on the night of the first full moon following the offence.'

Merlak's jaw dropped and he felt his senses swimming and his legs buckling as he tried to respond.

'The punishment for the male is to witness the execution of the female, and then to have his foobah surgically removed with a blunt stone axe without anaesthetic.' Liskae's father peered at Merlak over the top of his reading glasses. 'I believe most of the blokes chose to jump before the grandmothers arrived with the axes, if it's any comfort to you.'

Merlak fainted, but a grandmother quickly revived him with a pungent infusion of devil weed held under his nose. He looked up.

'How can you stand there so calmly and sentence your own daughter to death?'

'I told you this would be difficult for both of us, Merlak. But you did not let me finish my reading. There is an escape clause.'

Merlak sat up attentively. The page turned and the reading continued.

'Where the offenders are betrothed at the time of the offence, or where they are clearly so in love that this can be inferred then the normal punishments will not apply so long as the male can pass the test.'

'What test is this, sir? I will do anything to save Liskae.'

'I hope you will, boy. I am powerless now. Only you can save her, but the task is not as easy as it sounds.'

'And what is the test, sir? Juggling? Mathematics? Balancing on one leg? I am tolerably good at all of these things.'

'No, Merlak. The test is to spend one night alone in the

middle of the Snow Desert and to return to the village the next morning.'

'Well how hard can that be? I've done plenty of camping in my time. Let's get on with it and then Liskae will be free to marry me.'

'Not so fast, Merlak. Listen to me well, for my daughter's life depends on it. This challenge has not been faced for more than fifty years. Many went into the desert. Very few returned. Those who did spoke of terrible mirages and temptations that stretched their minds to the limit. Some of them were never whole men again. And none of them would talk in detail of their experiences.'

A grandfather stepped forward. 'I was a foobah fondler many years ago. I was sent to the desert and I returned. I will tell the boy all I know so that he may return safely and take Liskae's hand in marriage.'

And so that was how Merlak ended up listening to the deranged twitterings of the little grandfather for several days prior to ending up in the middle of the Glatchian Snow Desert.

The ancient fellow's basic premise was that if anything or anybody attempted to communicate with Merlak during the hours of darkness he must resist them. He had also given detailed guidance on the uses of devil weed, and had set Merlak several written tests to make sure that he had been listening.

Quite honestly it was a relief to be alone in the desert at last, and free from the constant stream of advice.

Liskae's suspended death sentence cast a shadow over everything, but Merlak could not believe that he would not succeed. He had modern equipment to protect him from the elements, and the devil weed urine ring was supplemented by ground radar and roving cam surveillance. His only weapon was a short keen-edged stabbing sword, but he did not expect to have to use it.

He pulled a picture of Liskae from his inner pocket and stared at it rapturously. 'I will not fail you, my darling.'

As darkness began to fall he zipped himself into his sleeping shelter and snuggled into his pod. Low-level radar and cam contacts relayed alerts to his handset. Just small nocturnal creatures moving around in search of even smaller nocturnal creatures. Nothing to worry about.

And then it was morning.

He awoke with a start and unzipped the shelter. He didn't remember falling asleep, but clearly he was still here and had passed the test.

He let out a whoop and stepped out into the daylight.

There in front of him was Liskae's father, his face a mask of grief.

'What's wrong, sir? See! I am here. I am alive. We must return home and free her!'

'You idiot, Merlak. She is dead. A week has passed. Why didn't you come back?'

'A week? No! That cannot be. My love cannot be dead!'

'Be a man, Merlak. Draw your sword and do the honourable thing.'

Merlak's hand seemed to move of its own accord to the hilt of the short sword. He drew it, then summoning all his will threw it at Liskae's father. It passed straight through him and as it did so his likeness rippled like a pond disturbed by a stone, and the Glatchian night was suddenly all around him again.

He hurried back to his shelter. There were still several hours of darkness left, and larger animals were being picked up by his sensors. But now that he was attuned to the real danger he could feel the weird beings probing his mind, seeking weaknesses.

He pulled out the picture again and placed it against his heart. 'I will not fail you, my darling.'

Attacks came and went during the night. People he knew. People he didn't know and would hope never ever to meet. Monsters and constructs from the depths of his fertile imagination. Each one wore him down a little more, but he clung to the thought of his Liskae.

And with each manifestation the beings seemed to become more real, more able to hold their shape under attack. But through the power of his will and his love for Liskae he beat them back and consigned them to the shadows they had crawled from.

Just before dawn, she came to him. He had known she must.

'My brave Merlak. Come to me, my love.'

Was it really her? Surely this could be no phantasm.

He started towards her, arms outstretched. 'You look so real, my love...'

'I am realer than real, Merlak. I am all your deepest wants and desires.'

And it was true. This was not his Liskae. This was his perfect woman, and he was so tired now, and so in need of affection. He felt the last of his resistance ebbing and could only think of collapsing into this beautiful creature's arms, and sleeping with her forever.

They embraced tightly as only true lovers can do, and he felt his separate existence begin to peacefully fade away.

From somewhere in the depths of what remained of his being the voice of the little grandfather spoke to him. 'Now, Merlak. Do it now, before it is too late!'

Summoning the last of his willpower Merlak farted thunderously and collapsed unconscious even as the poison hit his eyes and nose. Devil weed residue may be harmless to Merlak's kind in urine, but in bodily gas it is a toxic irritant once released to the atmosphere. In an enclosed space it has even been known to cause death, but this is thankfully a very rare event.

The effect of the gas on the unnatural creatures of the Snow Desert night is however more extreme, immediately destroying their molecular bonding and dissolving them back to whence they came.

Merlak's eyes opened on a bright new morning.

He packed his possessions and set off for the village, leaving only his two remaining tins of baked beans to mark the location of his epic battle.

Tonia Bevins

ON THE GRADE II LISTING OF WHITTINGTON LODGE, BATTERSEA DOGS & CATS HOME

'Twas ten in the morning on Thursday last week
I was reading *The Guardian* some diversion to seek
when a story leapt out and smacked me in the face.
(Good news – as you'll hear – for the whole feline race.)
In old London Town, near the Isle of Dogs
(who get too much press anyway) some fortunate mogs
will inhabit a magnificent Grade II listed building,
all columns and porticos, plenty of gilding,
a lodge, named for Whittington, that well-known Dick.
If they find themselves homeless (whether healthy or sick).
they'll have physic and fish, central heating and beds
with pillows for resting their sweet furry heads.
O, residents of the fashionable district of Battersea,
rejoice in the knowledge you now live in Cattersea!

Shauna Leishman

CHESHIRE COUNTY FAIR

Stopping at the patch of grass that had been assigned to her, Janna sighed. Dang it, she thought, I've got a bad location again. Need to figure out how to bribe my way into a better place.

Eventually, Janna pulled herself out of the truck and began unloading boxes and tables. She had just dumped one box on the ground when she heard a distinctive 'oomph'.

Hello? she thought, did I just hear something?

Glancing around, she didn't see anyone, so shrugging, she continued on with her unpacking. Going around to the other side of the boxes, she bent down to move one and suddenly, a leprechaun leapt at her, grabbed her nose and twisted it fiercely.

'Youch!' screamed Janna, as she fell backward, landing on her backside. Eyeing the little creature warily, she rubbed her nose, as it stood glaring at her with his hands on his hips. She then became fascinated and moving onto her knees, bent towards him, asking, 'Who are you and what do you want?'

''Tis about time,' he replied. 'We arranged for you to get this area and then, when you show up, you grumble and throw a box on me.'

'You arranged? What? Why would you arrange for me to get this spot? It's isolated, I'm not going to get any customers, I won't have good traffic,' sputtered Janna.

'Exactly. You won't get the dross but you'll get only the right people, the ones who need you. We also needed to talk to you without snoopy big ears around. We are supposed to be invisible, remember?'

'Right, I've never actually seen one of you before – what are you – an elf? A fairy?'

The little man kicked at her knee 'I'm a leprechaun, you idiot! Why, oh why do I have to deal with the likes of you?'

'Uh, okay, I give up, you tell me,' Janna retorted.

'Apparently you are the one. The one who is to bring us back into existence. Back from the ancient myths where we've been lost, back to reality.'

'ME?!' squealed Janna. 'How do you figure that?'

'Don't you remember? A few years ago you were seeking us. You found our places, you were beginning to hear us, we were calling you, we were just about to make contact when you disappeared.'

'Oh yes,' mused Janna. 'I was getting pulled into the old magic, but it began to freak me out and then stuff happened and then I ended up buying my shop…'

'Yes, it took us awhile to find you. We had to put a curse on you so you'd come back to us, but so far you've avoided the consequences somehow. That's why we set this up, finally.'

'Curse? What curse? What have you done?' Now Janna was the angry one.

'Well, have you made any money? Have you ever reached the pot at the end of the rainbow?' he asked.

'No, I haven't. Is that because of you? I've worked and worked and loved my shop but no, the money just disappears into a black hole. It's quite desperate, actually. You did that to me?' she cried.

'You will get it, we'll show you the pot,' the leprechaun said soothingly. 'Just as soon as you return to your true purpose. It's time to give up your distraction and you need to come back to seeking us out. It will be good, I promise.'

Janna was completely lost for words. She stared at the little man with her mouth hanging open. Nodding his head three times, he touched his nose and disappeared. Dazed, Janna stumbled to her feet and stood unmoving for a long time until she heard a shout.

'Oi! You going to be moving that truck anytime soon?' yelled the grounds manager.

With that, the sights and sounds of Cheshire County Fair came crashing back into her senses. She turned to the man with a grin. 'No problem, five minutes,' as she went back to work, setting up her stand, readying it for service.

Liz Sandbach

FENLAND

I lift my face, buried in your tangled hair,
to whisper 'convolvulus', 'meadow grass', 'reeds' and 'fen'.
But you are locked into wide sky,
my private commentary seeping, sleepy, in,
with the slow slap-slapping of water
and the distant cra-ra-rack of a heron in flight.

This is what binds us now,
in mind and marsh and bog,
as pious as Our Lady's pilgrims,
as watchful as Hereward.

And with the August sun,
sudden from clouds,
the words of a song:
'Flavum, flavum. Dwondi, Dwondi.
Sol omnipotens.'

Mark Acton

Token for a Foundling

Goodbye my baby, my sweet child. Farewell. I shall count the days, the hours, the seconds 'til we meet.

I can feel myself being torn apart as you are lifted from my arms. The strength has gone from my legs and I can no longer stand. Yet my arms remain extended in front of me.

Goodbye my sweet, sweet child. Remember my face as I will remember your black eyes staring into my soul. Remember the sound of my voice singing gentle songs into your ears as I will remember your anxious cries mellowing to an easy purr. Remember my loving touch as I will remember your tiny hands clasped around my long finger.

Treasure this token and think of me. The wheel is like your life. May it propel you forward and onward, but it always comes back 'round to me. The string is the cord that binds us together. It bound you to me before you were born, and it binds us still.

Goodbye my baby.

I will see you again.

I just need time.

And a plan.

I will be the best mother any child has ever had.

We will have such adventures.

Goodbye my love.

Don't forget me. Never forget me.

David Bruce

GRAFFITI FLIGHT

He'd just bought the last three Rust-oleum spray cans from Joe's Pound shop when it hit him.

It might have been that dodgy lunchtime burger or maybe someone had spiked his Special Brew in the Barrel but whatever it was, his head was spinning. Not just spinning, expanding, shrinking, slipping and turning inside out; someone else's head on his shoulders; that was it. Someone else's head. Not his head, but whoever's head it was, it was pulling the rest of his body along the path towards home. On past the Lazy Booze, past the Trust Bank and the Bookies and on to the hoardings, those glorious hoardings, his gallery, his contribution to the world of art. All his frustrations and passions sprayed out in yards of graphic colour and design and now as he looked on to it they came to life. Exploded into a swirling mass of brilliant colours, moving letters and curlicues in an oily slippery cosmos. In the centre, an iridescent spinning vortex was sucking him into its core. Should he take flight or stay and be drawn into his own polychrome wonderland? His legs, if they were his legs, decided for him. His butt collided heavily with the wet paving slabs and he was drawn in on a new journey of discovery.

A headlong dash past yellow trees that wore babies for leaves. Cats as small as mice and mice as big as donkeys, all ploughing through a foaming sea of purple grasses. A Cinderella coach pulled alongside and he settled into its nest of orange feathers as it lifted off into the skies and floated up towards a grinning moon that morphed into a roaring lion's maw. Visceral fears choked in his throat and demanded *flight or fight – flight –* he dived through the feathers into the swirling sea below. A sea full of swimming monkeys that nipped and bit at his soft blue body.

Then flashes of the real world began to intrude, or was he already in his real world? He felt the wet pavement freezing his arse and new images began to flicker like the end of a cine film flapping through the projector gate.

Flick- Flick- Flick- A crowd was pressing in on him. Mostly people, but in hues he'd only seen on a Krylon colour chart. The jabbering, the sounds, what did they mean? Then there was a wailing, rising and falling getting louder and louder and pulsing blue lights coming for him. *Fight or flight – flight.* He pushed off the pavement, shook off the grasping hands and hurdled the two-metre hoarding, as if it was a match stick. Fleeing into the semi-solid trashed world of a back lot on a wet night in Blackburn. The coppers managed, somehow, to scramble over the hoardings and took off after him. He could hear their clamour as they waded through the empty tinnies, discarded detritus and his old Rust-oleum spray cannons. He looked back and *Flick- Flick- Flick-* he saw the biting monkeys chasing him again as he was ploughing through a sea of polystyrene burger boxes and coke cans behind Jerry's Grill. His feet crunching, crushing, dragging, tripping and then *Flick- Flick- Flick-* he was floating again and the green monkeys were gnashing at his heals. *Flight or fight?* He must choose. He looked down at his hands. *Flick- Flick- Flick-* He was a Transformer now, morphed and hungry for action, with steel hammers for hands; he was ready. He turned to face the green humanoids.

A loud pop and two yellow wires snaked out and struck his shoulder and a totally new experience began to unfold. A startling jolt, a powerful weakness and he lay amongst the rubbish, cramping and twitching before his world slipped into a swirling nebula, punctuated by exploding stars and graffiti so transcendental it could not have been drawn by any human hand. What was this supreme artist's Tag?

TASER MX-20.

Marian Smith

THE LUCK OF THE IRISH

I suppose that if I was destined to meet Josie O'Keefe again, it would be in a hospital A&E Department. She was the most accident-prone person I'd ever known. We first met when we were sixteen, a couple of giggling Saturday girls working in our local delicatessen.

Josie had an almost magnetic attraction for disaster. She had several close encounters with the bacon slicer, and knives falling to the floor would, like guided missiles, target her feet. And she was very selective in her trail of havoc; she would always drop whole trays of duck eggs (never one or two) and only the most expensive extra-virgin olive oil.

Called upon, before the shop opened one Saturday, to deal with a bluebottle that had expired in a window display full of continental cheese, Josie tackled the job with good humour, a bowl of hot water and a bottle of disinfectant. A passing ex-boyfriend knocked on the window, and a startled Josie knocked over the bowl of water, and replaced the pungent tones of Gorgonzola and Roquefort, with Tesco's own-brand pine disinfectant. This was the end of her short career in food retail. Saturdays were never quite the same after that.

You couldn't help but admire Josie, due to her cheerfulness in the face of disaster. The luck of the Irish was not something she inherited, but she had a total acceptance of what she saw as her own personal bad luck, and a complete faith in the fact that Things would pick up. However many times she dropped them.

She was sitting in the corner of the waiting room. As soon as I approached her, she leapt to her feet, and still managed a rib-cracking hug, despite holding one heavily-bandaged hand aloft. And I was instantly back in our student lodgings, sharing a bottle of cheap wine and a Chinese takeaway, along with the memory of Josie, whose friendship had been one of the few bright lights in my relentlessly gloomy teenage years.

Josie, who had raised my self-esteem, had sat with me till four in the morning listening to my troubles, even though she had never known the root of my misery. Josie, who had never questioned my love for my father, even though she must have questioned his bizarre rules and rituals.

Then, in the autumn following my nineteenth birthday, she moved to Birmingham; I began training to be a nurse, and somehow we lost touch with each other.

But here she was, sitting in A&E. It was New Year's Eve and, having drawn the short straw, I was on the night-shift, so we only had time for a brief chat as I had to leave and apply myself to the first batch of party revelers who were destined to throw up over me. We exchanged phone numbers and she said I must come round for a meal so we could catch up.

Now, when they were handing out the instinct for self-preservation, I got Josie's ration, so my first reaction was to make an excuse for passing up on this offer, as I was convinced that, if her talent for disaster extended to the kitchen, I would be lucky to escape with a minor case of botulism.

I started making some 'I wouldn't want to put you to any trouble, why don't we go out for a meal' sort of noises, when she said 'Oh but you must come round, Sean is coming over on Saturday and he and my boyfriend will be there for supper so we could make up a foursome.'

Sean, her beautiful older brother, would be there. There was no hesitation. I pretended to mentally check my diary, announced I was free and accepted. We exchanged phone numbers, said our goodbyes and I left her in the waiting room.

For the rest of that night shift, it was hard to take my mind off Sean O'Keefe, who had been the object of my love and wanting for the most of my teenage years. It was a sad sort of wanting, for I doubt he saw me as anything other than one of his little sister's friends.

The Sean O'Keefe I remembered was a major draw for a single girl (and probably several married ones), and was known among my female acquaintances as Lust at First Sight, and with good reason. Sean had dark brown eyes, framed with obscenely long eyelashes. He had a perfect face, tanned skin and bleached-blond hair; he had long legs and his jeans looked like they had been spray-painted onto his arse. He was charming and witty; you could have taken him home to your mother, but of course, you wouldn't because your mother might take a fancy to him as well, and you couldn't risk the competition.

But then by chance, one of my sad teenage dreams came true. My last encounter with Sean O'Keefe was when he kissed me after a Christmas party at exactly 2:17 in the morning. I was stunned by this unexpected gift. In later years I would squirm at the recollection, but I ran into the toilet, trying desperately not to lick my lips, pressed them onto a piece of loo paper, then folded the blessed relic carefully and hid it in my handbag.

I carried this treasure with me everywhere, and kept it for six months, until I inadvertently grabbed it following a sudden nosebleed. The imprint of my lips, which had touched his lips for that brief, glorious moment, disappeared into a glob of nasal blood. It was on the night of my eighteenth birthday and I was gutted. But I couldn't share this pain, not even with Josie, who had no idea how I felt about her brother.

It has been six years since I'd seen Sean. Josie told me he was working as a stockbroker in the City now, and that he was still single. There was no way I was going to let an opportunity like this slip away. God knows, I needed something good to happen in my life, and in walks Sean O'Keefe. It had to be fate.

I walked up the front path of Josie's house, an Edwardian terrace in north London. There was no doubt that I had come to the right place. It was just as neat and tidy as her neighbour's, but it was the cracked pane of glass in the front door and the sign reading 'Bell doesn't work, please knock' that advertised the fact that Josie lived there.

I could hear music coming from the back of the house. I hammered on the door, and several minutes later the music stopped, the door opened and Josie was there, a broad grin upon her face. She was dressed in jeans and a man's shirt, splattered with stains in every shade from madras curry to red wine. Her long chestnut hair was tied at the nape of her neck but several strands had escaped and she kept pushing them out of her eyes with her still bandaged hand.

I suddenly felt overdressed. I had changed my outfit a dozen times before I had settled on this smart black dress; it was my most subtle and sophisticated 'get your man' outfit.

Almost as if she could read my mind she said, 'My you look lovely, I'd better get properly dressed before the lads arrive. Alex is picking Sean up on his way over. I'm just finishing off in the kitchen, come through and we can have a chat and a glass of wine.'

Alex. What a pity. I'd always hated the name, or rather, its associations. Alex Baker, who had bullied me at school. Alex Grenville, who had taken up the drums after Pa and I had moved into the flat below his. And then there was… I brought myself mentally back into Josie's kitchen.

It was surprisingly neat and tidy. The only evidence that this was Josie's kitchen was a cookery book that was almost as stained as her shirt, with corners that were brown and scorched, as if she had used it to beat out a fire. I was comforted to notice that there was a fire extinguisher attached to the wall. She must have seen me looking at it.

'Alex told me I had to buy that,' she explained, 'given my track record.'

I smiled. 'And how many times have you used it?'

She grinned. 'Only the once, after the recipe book wasn't up to the job.'

'So tell me about Alex.'

She looked wistful. 'We met in a bookshop a couple of months ago. Surprise, surprise, I stepped on his foot.'

'And he still asked you out?'

'Well, not straight away. He moved out of my way, and we demolished a pile of chick lit.'

'So he's accident prone as well then?'

'Not a bit, he can't afford to be, he works for a security

firm in Leicester.'

'That's a long way away,' I said. 'Do you get to see him very often?'

'Not as much as I'd like, but it makes it more special when we are together. I feel so lucky, I can't believe he asked me out. I thought he was way out of my league, but here I am, dating this gorgeous guy. Even Sean approves of him, says he's a great improvement on most of the men I've dated, and you know what he's like, still playing the protective brother.'

Of course, while she was telling me about the new love of her life, all I could do was listen out for the front door bell that would herald the arrival of the main event. Josie stood up and announced she was going upstairs to get dressed. She ushered me into the living room and told me to make myself at home.

A wood fire crackled, and there was a pungent smell of hot spice and the warm pine needles from the Christmas tree. The room exuded an air of old-fashioned elegance and homeliness. I was just looking at her collection of books when there was a voice behind me.

'It's a pretty boring selection isn't it?'

I spun round. Sean O'Keefe stood in the open doorway. He was taller than I remembered him, his hair now seemed a sort of mousy colour, but his eyes were as dark and as lovely as ever. His skin was pale, as if he had stayed out of the sun for too long. But the voice was still deep, and seemed to resonate across the room.

I suppose he must have seen me blushing. 'Don't worry, it's not like I caught you nicking the silver.' He grinned. I was about to melt into a puddle of incoherent rambling when he said over his shoulder, 'Alex, come and meet Roz.'

The man called Alex walked in behind Sean.

I don't know why people say that they freeze. I didn't. A wave of hot fear washed over me from head to foot, then came back up again and solidified in the pit of my stomach. I felt dizzy and sick and very hot and cold at the same time.

I fixed my eyes on Sean, so that he would assume he was the cause of my wide eyed horror.

'Sorry,' he said. 'I didn't mean to make you jump.'

I muttered some sort of apology, but he seemed oblivious to my intense embarrassment, and before I could say anything else, he blundered on, and announced to Alex that he hadn't seen me since that Christmas party where, he grinned, 'I kissed this lovely young lady and she promptly ran into the bog, presumably to throw up. I was going to ask her to dance, but bottled out then. Fine dent to my pride that was, I can tell you.'

Even in the midst of my fear and confusion, the last remark was not lost upon me, and I realised in those few seconds that Sean had remembered that night and remembered me; this was followed by the sudden awful realisation that if I'd stayed where I was, instead of running into the toilet, he might even have asked me for a date. Then the Alex situation came thundering right back to the front of my thoughts.

Sean must have thought that the appalled expression on my face was due entirely to my being reminded of this pathetic episode. I forced myself to look at Alex again. The colour had also drained away from his face, but he seemed to be making a supreme effort to gather his wits, and smiled weakly at Sean.

'Then it serves you right and shame on you for reminding her about it. Now before you make matters worse, why don't you go and find out what's keeping Josie from her visitors, while Roz and I get to know each other.'

Get to know each other. I thought I was going to throw up. Sean disappeared in the direction of the kitchen. An awful gaping silence descended on the room.

Alex went to the door, glanced down the hall, and then pushed it almost shut. He crossed the room and stood in front of me, his face uncomfortably close to mine. I was aware of being trapped against the bookcase, his six foot frame between me and the door. He leant over me, and spoke very softly. He actually looked afraid.

'Do they know about you? About your father?'

I opened my mouth but no words came out. I shook my head.

'OK, now listen to me. We have never met. You do not

know me, you do not make any reference to anything I may have done in the past and you do not ask any questions at all. Do you understand?'

I just stared at him. 'Do you understand?' he repeated, only this time, there was a threat in his voice. I nodded.

'You will begin to feel unwell, and leave as soon as it's reasonable to do so. Is that clear?'

I nodded again.

'Good,' he whispered. 'And in return for your discretion, your private life is your own business. But if you dare slip up... well, I think you understand the consequences.' He paused, took a deep audible breath, and then continued. 'Now, I suggest we start chatting about the weather.'

The first sound I was able to make was half way between a gasp and a sob. As he went back across the room to open the door again, I rediscovered the power of speech.

'Wait,' I whispered. 'What are you doing here? What's going on?'

He stopped, sighed, looked at the floor and then turned slowly back at me. 'I can't tell you, and even if I could, I wouldn't.'

His arrogance unsettled me; I wanted to go on the attack, for all my pitiful stock of ammunition. 'Like I'm no good at keeping secrets?'

'Only your own,' he hissed.

'It looks like you have secrets to keep now.'

He turned on me, once more asserting his physical presence. 'Don't even think about threatening me!'

'That wasn't a threat, just a statement of fact. This must be some sort of undercover job, so that means that you think she's a criminal.'

'Josie? A criminal? Don't be so stupid!'

I suddenly felt very ridiculous for assuming that of the two of them, it was Josie he was spying on.

We both heard the voices outside at the same time. I immediately turned my back on the door and pretended to look at the record collection. I needed as much time as possible to pull myself back into some semblance of normality.

Alex sat on the sofa and looked completely relaxed. His composure angered me even more. 'You're very good at this, aren't you,' I thought. 'You must do this all the time.'

Josie walked into the room; I could only admire the transformation. She had changed into a dark red long-sleeved dress, with a deep neckline showing a subtle hint of cleavage. It fitted every curve perfectly. She wore no jewelry, so emphasising her pale skin and chestnut hair.

'You look lovely,' I whispered.

She beamed in appreciation, but it was obvious she was only interested in what Alex thought.

'Yes, you look very beautiful,' he said, once more in total command of the situation.

She responded with a blush and an expression of total adoration that only made me feel more wretched and angry. Poor vulnerable Josie, it was all going to go wrong for her again.

'Shall we eat?' she said.

I am not sure how I managed to eat that meal, my mouth was dry. Josie had made a beef casserole, liberally laced with red wine. The heady smell filled the room. It was, without a doubt, an impressive culinary achievement, but my appetite had gone, replaced by the knot in my stomach.

I couldn't take my eyes off Sean. I tried to reassess him in the light of this new information, but he persisted in being as charming and witty as I remembered him. Sometimes I caught him looking at me, and he blushed but held my gaze. I had captured his interest at last. And I knew I would have to walk away.

Without even looking at him, I was aware that Alex was observing this silent conversation between us, and that he didn't like what he saw. I took some small comfort in witnessing his agitation.

Then, while clearing away the empty plates, Josie said, 'Oh, I forgot to ask, how's your Pa doing these days?'

I can't imagine what she thought the reason was for my

blushing at this innocent question. I played for time by pretending I hadn't heard her question. She looked confused, but repeated it.

'Not good, his asthma is much worse these days, takes a dozen different tablets a day, you know how it is. How are your mum and dad, still living in Harrow?'

I'd never even met her parents, and I saw Josie and Sean glance at each other and then back to me. But I didn't care; the subject had been diverted onto safer ground.

During the meal, Sean tried to keep filling our wine glasses. I refused, I needed to stay sober so that I could concentrate on the getting the small talk right. Alex had the excuse that he was driving. At the third attempt to refill my glass, I said, 'Well actually, I have rather a headache.' I glanced at Alex and I saw a hint of a nod.

I declined offers of aspirin, and said that I was very sorry, but would they mind if I rang for a taxi. Sean immediately stood up and said he would take me home.

'It's OK, I'll go,' said Alex. 'You've had a couple of glasses of wine, can't be too careful these days.'

Josie was about to protest, but he leant down, and kissed her on the top of her head. 'Don't worry my love, the roads are quiet. I'll be back in under an hour.'

Sean looked disappointed. He shot me a glance that said 'I'll call you.' All I could do was smile politely. He suggested that Alex should go and get his car and drive it round to the front of the house so that I wouldn't have to walk out far in the rain. Alex said it wasn't necessary; the car was less than a minute's walk away. I knew he wasn't going to leave us alone together.

I hugged Josie, and she said I must come round again. I said I would look forward to that, feeling desolate at the necessity of this lie. We walked out into the rain in silence and got into Alex's car; he was about to speak when I cut in.

'Quite a promotion for you then, from lackey in the Witness Protection service to undercover policeman, or should it be professional liar?'

I was gratified to see he looked uncomfortable. 'I don't enjoy this part of the job; it's just the way it has to be sometimes. It's unfortunate, but I really don't have a choice.'

'And what about Josie? I can see she's besotted by you. Do you care about her, or is she just an unfortunate part of the job as well?'

'Yes, as a matter of fact that's just what she is. But if you must know, I do care what happens to her. She's a nice kid, and I don't want her to get hurt, but then, I don't want other people to get hurt either. There are times when you have to make hard choices. I thought you at least would understand that.'

'Meaning?'

'You know exactly what I mean. It would have been a lot easier for your father to do a stretch in prison than to enter the witness protection programme. He did that for you.'

I could barely contain my anger. 'And of course, let's not forget what he did for you.'

'You sound bitter,' he said quietly.

'Damn right I'm bitter,' I snapped. 'But not with my father. With you bastards, you treated us like dirt.'

'For Christ's sake, Roz, grow up! What did you expect, our undying admiration? Your father was a criminal. He gave us the names we needed; we gave him a new identity. That was the deal. It was never going to be an easy relationship for either side.'

I couldn't respond to that, and he knew it.

'Listen to me Roz, your father was protecting you, and it's your turn to protect him now. So let's get this clear. If Sean O'Keefe phones you, under no circumstances must you arrange to see him again.'

He would never know what that meant for me. In the course of one night, to have come so close and then to lose the one thing that I had wanted for so many years.

He must have thought that I had not absorbed what he had said, so he repeated it.

'Roz, did you hear me, you mustn't make contact with him again.'

Suddenly, I felt quite calm. If Sean O'Keefe was going to

disappear out of my life, I wanted reasons.

'Are you going to tell me why? Let's face it, I know enough already. If I was to go and tell him that you are one of the Met's finest, I think you'd be sunk anyway, so nothing you could tell me will make it any worse for you.'

'It could make it worse for you though.'

'I doubt it.'

There was urgency in his voice. 'Believe me, Roz, a little knowledge can be a dangerous thing. Supposing Sean found out that you knew exactly what he was involved in, what do you think he would do? Take my advice, walk away.'

I was grasping for some reason to justify my feelings. There was something about the way he said 'what he was involved in' that convinced me that Sean couldn't be a master criminal, that, like Pa, he had got dragged in to something that was too big for him to control.

'Sean can't be dangerous.'

'Are you sure? Do you really want to take that chance?'

I said nothing. I knew he was right. And I knew that for Pa's sake, I couldn't afford to take any risks. Somehow though, I didn't want to give him the satisfaction of hearing me say the words. The police had cast a shadow over my family life. The desire to do damage was very strong. I wanted him to feel the fear for as long as possible, just as Pa had. I didn't want to make any promises. But Alex wouldn't let it go.

'You must stay away from him, Roz. For your own sake, and your father's. I need to know that you aren't going to cause me any problems.'

'OK, but I'm keeping quiet for my father, not for you.'

He must have heard the defeat in my voice. 'That's good enough.'

He started the engine and we moved off.

'You can drop me off at the station; I'll make my own way from there.'

'No, I said I'd take you home, so I have to do just that, otherwise I'll get back too soon.'

I didn't argue; there wasn't any point. We drove on in

silence. Twenty minutes later, as I got out of the car, he said 'I'm sorry to hear that your father is ill.'

Damn him, damn his mock concern. I didn't answer, but just slammed the door and glared at him contemptuously. He wound down the window. 'You won't be hearing from me again unless I hear that you've changed your mind.'

I said nothing. I walked slowly up the path, opened the front door and pushed it shut behind me without looking back. After three or four minutes I heard the car pull away.

I stood there, my head throbbing. They'd had their pound of flesh ten years ago, and Pa had been watching over his shoulder ever since. As if a change of identity means you can sleep at night. It doesn't, it just means the nightmares don't come so often, but they still come. I heard them, every time.

Although I was still shaking, I knew Pa must have heard me come in, so I went straight into the living room to say goodnight. He was sitting, hunched up in his chair, his head resting on his chest. On the table beside him, there was a glass of whisky and his asthma inhaler. He was quiet. I listened for the usual wheezing but heard none. I became aware that the room was intensely cold.

'Pa,' I said, 'you've let the fire go out.' He was always such a light sleeper, but he said nothing. A sudden feeling of panic shot through me. I touched his hand; it was cold. I knelt down beside him and looked into his eyes. They stared into the hearth. Mechanically, I felt for his pulse.

I must have sat beside him for about ten minutes. I knew I should call an ambulance but I couldn't move. Finally, I forced myself back on my feet and picked up the phone, but only got as far as the second 9 and put the receiver back down. Then I picked it up again and dialled.

It rang for four or five times before Josie answered.

'Hi, it's me, Roz. Is Alex back yet?'

'No, but he rang to say he was on his way. He'll be here in ten minutes. Is something the matter?'

'No, nothing at all. Just go and tell Sean to come to the phone.'

Linda Leigh

AFTERNOON NAP

A tiny hand crunched up tight
You rub your eyes, not yet it isn't night
I smiled gently at you, we both knew
It was time for that afternoon curfew

We climbed the stairs together you and I
Look at me go up so high
You giggled as your hands found the way
Please don't fall backwards I pray
Knees and toes follow your fun
At last the top step and then you run

We play and chat, just you and I
Then you look and we both know
It's time to put your head down for a while
My heart beats fast as I pick you up and smile

We try the cot first but then you cry
I talk some more, you hold Ellie and sigh
Walk away, 'uddle, uddle' you shout
So back I come and lift you out

We sit on the rocking chair and read a book
You gaze at me with one last look
Legs and toes curl around my waist
Arms and head rest on my chest

Facing forward, snuggled down, two hearts beating fast
Instant sleep, a tender moment stilled the moment forever to last
I held you tight and felt inside of me a sudden rush
Like the feeling of heat when you suddenly blush

There is no photograph I can take
That captures what we make
Just a moment of time within our day
When no words were needed to say

Two hearts beating on so fast
This time is magic it cannot last
I savour the peace and what you are
Whilst singing softly 'Twinkle, twinkle little star'

Bill Webster

ARTEFACT

The rain came out of nowhere. After the sexual athletics with Karen last night, Jim had intended having a relaxing morning in town before meeting Linda for lunch and a little afternoon love. He had just indulged his desire for an unhealthy McDonald's breakfast and was now heading on towards the city centre.

Then the rain came, a heavy shower that threatened to soak him and spoil the rest of his day. Unless Linda would maybe go for the drowned rat look? He chuckled to himself as he ducked into the first available shop doorway.

The old-style bell above the door chimed to announce his presence as he surveyed his surroundings. He was standing on a well-worn dark-stained wooden floor ... not that much of it was visible. Counters and tables and shelves and various contrivances covered almost every available inch of floorspace, leaving only a small meandering gangway for the would-be customer to negotiate. There was an ancient quality to the light in the shop as if there was an ethereal plankton bloom drifting between the reefs formed by the bookshelves and the arrangements on the sales tables. For just a moment he caught his breath, feeling that he could drown in here.

He turned to leave the shop but saw the rain still hammering down onto the pavement outside, and hesitated. And then the man was there. He must have entered silently from a back room or something, because he had not been there a moment ago. To Jim's eye he looked like something out of a Dickens novel, archaically dressed in blue doublet and brown hose with a night-black cape reaching almost to the ankles of his stout leather boots. His long grey hair and beard were more Tolkien than Dickens, but his piercing blue eyes blazed with an energy and intensity that belied his advanced years.

Jim suddenly realised that he had been staring at the man slack-jawed like a beached fish and moved towards him to cover his embarrassment.

'What an amazing place you have here.'

The man smiled and gave a barely perceptible bow. 'Thank you, sir. We pride ourselves on having something of interest for everyone ... and also on offering shelter from the elements.'

He laughed then, and Jim was not at all sure that it was a laugh that he ever wanted to hear again.

'It is all right, sir. Excuse an old man's little joke. You are very welcome here, and many of our best customers have found us in exactly the manner that you have just done.'

Jim made to protest but the old man raised his hand.

'No matter how you found us. The important thing is that you are here now, and that your item is calling to you. Please, take your time and look around. I will be here if you need any help.'

Jim felt he ought to respond in some way to this strangely dressed man with his unique style of sales patter, but no words came and so he just smiled a 'thank you' to the shopkeeper and turned to inspect the items on display.

He noticed in passing that it was bright and sunny outside again and that there was not the slightest sign that there had ever been any rain. You just had to love the vagaries of the British weather.

Anyhow, five minutes politely looking round the shop and then he would say his goodbyes and be out of this odd place. His mind turned to other things and he found himself formulating a mental scorecard rating Karen and Linda and Sue and Naomi on their attributes and capabilities. He sighed with regret that he could not include Jayne on the list. She had been so good in bed but had been so unreasonable when she found out about Karen.

'Are you alright, sir? Did you say something?'

'Sorry, no. I was just thinking of something that made me a

little sad. I'm OK now, thank you.'

'As you please. Look further and I am sure we will find an item that will ease your sadness.'

He tried to shut the girls out of his mind and concentrated on the stuff in the shop. He supposed it was meant to be an antiques or collectables store, but there seemed to be some real junky stuff among the items. Classy-looking statuettes and china sat alongside nondescript electrical goods. And there were things that seemed very modern. He picked up a silver palm-sized object that looked like a flip phone and pressed the button on the side. It sprung open with a chirruping sound revealing a high-definition colour screen and a miniature keypad.

Jim couldn't resist it. 'Beam me up, Scotty!'

A wizened hand closed on his. 'Better not to fool around with some of these artefacts, sir. The results can be unpredictable.'

'Oh, come on. It's only a stage prop for goodness sake.'

'We do not deal in 'stage props', sir. Everything in this shop is the genuine item.'

Jim supposed that age and hanging around in this place had earned the old man the right to a modicum of madness and started to make his way towards the door and normality.

'Would you like her back, sir?'

Jim stopped with his hand on the doorknob and turned to face the shopkeeper. 'I beg your pardon?'

'I said, would you like her back? The one you were thinking about a moment ago? The one who has made you sad?'

'Who put you up to this? How do you know about Jayne? Who the hell are you?'

'My young friend ... Who I am and how I know does not matter. You have one chance here today to change your life. Once you step out of that door, my shop will move on and you will never find it again. If you want to change your life, then you must suspend your disbelief and take the chance I am offering you.'

Jim looked through the grimy shop window at the scene of

normality outside and tried to think back to the many times he had walked past this spot.

'Your shop feels like it has been here forever, and yet I never saw it before today.'

'My shop is a travelling shop. It is drawn to those who need it. Take your chance my young friend, or forever regret its passing.'

The old man bent down behind his counter and stood with a blue ring box in his hands. He blew the dust from it and handed it to Jim.

'The ring of Cetompeni. Crafted for one of the first pharaohs. Wear this ring, James Royle, and any woman will be smitten by you.'

'A magic ring!' Jim choked off the derisory words that wanted to escape from his mouth and hurt the old man. Instead he opened the box to see a pale gold ring with hieroglyphic characters etched on both the inside and the outside of the band. It had a genuine look of antiquity about it, but it was only when he touched it and felt the joy and calm coursing through his body that he realised there really were more things in heaven and earth than he had ever contemplated.

He looked up in awe at the old man. 'It's a magic fucking ring ...'

The old man looked satisfied. 'This is the item that called you, James Royle. Put the ring on your finger, and your life will never be the same again.'

Jim looked hungrily at the ring in the palm of his hand. 'But I could never afford this. It must be priceless.'

The old man smiled. 'Indeed, it is priceless, but the items in this shop are not purchased with anything as base as money. Put the ring on your finger, James. Go and retrieve your Jayne.'

The ring slid onto his finger and was a perfect fit. He pulled his gaze away from it and looked up at the old man. 'So, is this some kind of Faustian pact? Will you be coming back for my soul?'

The old man smiled reassuringly. 'No, James. The ring

provides its own balance. You will attract all the women you desire. And the ring will take what it needs from you. You owe me nothing. Now go to your Jayne. My shop is being called by its next customer.'

The old man smiled and opened the door for Jim who mumbled his thanks and stepped outside. And suddenly he was outside Timpsons. It had been a Timpsons for years. He held onto the door jamb to steady himself as the disorientation washed over him.

One of the staff came to the door. 'You all right, mate?'

Jim took a deep breath and willed himself to stop trembling. 'Yeah. I'm OK now, thanks.' He smiled. 'Just a bit of a dizzy turn. Didn't get much sleep last night.' He gave his helper a little salute and headed up the road towards his lunch date with Linda. He glanced at his watch and saw the flash of gold on his ring finger and had to stop again to gather himself. Had it really happened? He glanced around him and was conscious that he seemed to be the centre of attraction. Women of all ages were casting coy and not-so-coy glances in his direction.

Was it really true?

He pulled out his mobile and sent a text cancelling his appointment with Linda, then called Jayne.

'You've got a nerve ...' she started, and then just tailed off.

Jim spoke into the silence. 'I really need to see you, Jayne. I need to see you now, please.'

He heard nervous breathing at the other end of the call. Then she spoke. 'You sound different, Jim. God forgive me, but all of a sudden I really need to see you too. Come round to the flat quickly before I change my mind.'

Jim grinned and ended the call.

He would get Jayne back. He could hear it in her voice. And judging by the reactions of the women around him, the ring would let him have any woman he wanted. The old man had been right.

It would normally have taken fifteen minutes to get to Jayne's but Jim made it in ten. There were some things she could do that put her right at the top of his scorecard, and he was looking forward to reacquainting himself with them.

She virtually dragged him through the door and within a minute they were in her bed. Five minutes later they sat companionably together.

'Don't worry about it, Jim. It happens to all men from time to time. Just stress or an infection or something. I love you so much.'

'Maybe if you try that trick of yours again,' he suggested.

But another five minutes later she sat up and said, 'Sorry Jim, I just need a little rest. And trying too hard is just going to make things worse for you.'

She held his hand and her fingers stroked over the ring. 'What an interesting ring! Can I see it?'

Jim went to take the ring off, but it would not budge. It was not so much that it was tight – more that it seemed to have welded itself to his skin.' He shrugged to Jayne in defeat.

So she examined it in situ, running her finger in fascination over the etched characters.

'It's lovely Jim. Where did you get it?'

Jim smiled at her enthusiasm despite his flaccidity. 'In a funny little shop this morning. Apparently it used to belong to a pharaoh and it's called the Ring of Cetompeni.'

Jayne's brow furrowed for a moment and then she giggled.

He smiled down at her. 'What's so funny?'

'Oh nothing, Jim. Your pharaoh's name just struck me as being like a crossword clue, that's all.'

'Like a clue? How is it like a clue?'

'Well, it's an anagram, but now isn't the best time … honestly, Jim.'

'Oh, come on, Jayne! Don't be a tease. What is it?'

'OK. But it's a silly thing, Jim. Just one of these silly coincidences. If you rearrange the letters of Cetompeni, it spells impotence.' She smiled up at his suddenly pale face and kissed his lips. 'See, just a silly thing.'

Liz Leech

WALKING IN THE GROUNDS OF HAWARDEN CASTLE

Stepping through the red door into solitude
A wide vista gives free rein to the rhythms
Beating out nature with an even pulse.
Time stands still, yet draws one backwards.
Branches stretch down to entwine each other
In a long tender embrace,
Whilst others reach out towards the sun.
Oaks, sentinels of the path, watch our progress,
As they have watched countless footfalls before.
Bright green fungi highlight their branches
Set against deep red withies and buds of another species.
Shallow roots of beech slide down the moat-side,
Clasping earth to retain their position,
Seeking succour amongst the decaying undergrowth.
Discarded oak leaves, large as saucers,
Gather with those of beech, lime and hornbeam.
They nurture tiny plants,
Harbingers of springtime flowers.
The ruined castle, like the trees,
Looks down upon a timeless,
Yet ever-changing landscape.
Its stones are wise, hewn by a long-forgotten hand,
Fashioned into a defensive structure
That has spanned the centuries.
Nature is ever present. 'Watch me,' she cries,
'As I have been watched before.
As I am watching you now.'
We are not alone in such a landscape.
If we stood still, would we hear the earth move?
Would we see the grains turn over

As they tumble down the molehill's side?
Would those somehow primeval creatures
Be careless enough to expose their burrowing paws?
Pink nose. Dark close-cropped fur
Slides through unseen tunnels.
Do our footsteps mask the sound
Of earthworms and dinner?
Yet sometimes their mounds march side by side
With our pathways, egging us on.
Some tumble down slopes in a haphazard jumble
Or congregate around tree roots.
'How deep is your tunnel, mole?
When you push upward a bright red clay mound
Beside one of a darker loam,
Have you been travelling
Through different strata of time?
Will you nudge up a Roman coin,
Or a shard of Neolithic pottery
As you travel towards repletion?'
And yet...
You missed one!
A small thin convulsing be-ringed thing.
Cast up, who knows how,
Upon the cracked Tarmacadam path,
Desperately seeking a soft yielding haven.
I hear no birds, yet they are there,
Awaiting their chorus at eventide.
I see no voles, yet they are there,
Passing their short lives
Making runs beneath the rotting autumn spillage.
How many of us reach up to the sky for benediction,
When others turn their backs upon exposure
To seek refuge in darkness
In order to live another day?

David H. Varley

KINGDOM COME

We hear about the end of war,
The news is sung from door to door,
While bodies pile up on the floor
And all our feelings numb.
O Lord, O Lord,
Is this thy kingdom come?

The statues went and towers fell,
We were told all would be well,
The Devil sighs and reigns in hell
Atop a growing sum.
O Lord, O Lord,
Is this thy kingdom come?

A lonely rider rides the sky,
White horse, white drone, away to fly,
But we aground must love and die
Beneath a ruler's thumb.
O Lord, O Lord,
Is this thy kingdom come?

Did John alone have eyes that see?
Can one be both a slave and free?
The laws that govern you and me
Do not apply to some.
O Lord, O Lord,
Is this thy kingdom come?

All bodies rise up from the ground,
And march to here from all around,
They only hear the trumpet's sound,

The beating of a drum.
O Lord, O Lord,
Is this thy kingdom come?

And they have died that yet do live,
Poor souls with nothing left to give,
That cannot damn, that can't forgive
But only can succumb.
O Lord, O Lord,
Is this thy kingdom come?

We tools of war were made to mar,
In Father's fire we sear and char,
So never knowing what we are
Nor what we may become.
O Lord, O Lord,
This is thy kingdom come.

Shantele Janes

MEMORIES

She lay in bed staring at the familiar ceiling. Or at least it used to seem familiar. Something felt different, not as it should be, but she couldn't put her finger on it. The morning sun peered through the crack in the curtains, creating shadowy figures on the peeling artex. Maybe that's all it was, a trick of the light. Maybe if her eyesight were what it was forty years ago. She paused for a second to think. No, she was sure there was something. Of course – the light shade – that was it. Who had changed the light shade? A stark white circular paper lantern hung above her head. That wasn't a proper light shade; it looked like something her son had had in the '70s. *Her* light shade was made of crimson damask and it had tassles. It was a proper light shade. And someone had stolen it.

'George…' she whispered, still motionless, staring at this alien object that had invaded the room.

But there was no response.

'George,' she repeated, an urgency now in her voice.

Still no response.

She turned over, expecting to see the sleep-crumpled face of her husband beside her, but instead a smooth, undented pillowcase lay where his balding head should have been. Her initial thought was that he had gone downstairs, or was pottering about the garden as he often did on Sunday mornings, but something niggled inside of her and she sensed that this wasn't the case. She cast her eyes around the room again. It wasn't just the light shade that seemed different and unfamiliar, but everything else too. It was their room, she was sure of that, but it felt like someone had sneaked in overnight and replaced all of their belongings with a stranger's. The wallpaper was gone, replaced with a smooth green paint, the antique set of drawers she had been given by her sister had morphed into a pine dresser and where was the mirror she bought last week? Then suddenly it struck her – where were George's things? His favourite green cardigan that he always left on top of the wash basket, his brown suede slippers she had bought him for his birthday, the aftershave he saved for special occasions? But more importantly, where was his wallet? George always left his wallet on top of the drawers, always. By now she was sitting upright in the bed and she could hear her heart drumming through her ears. She reached out clumsily for her tablets on the bedside cabinet and spilt their contents all over the eiderdown.

'Calm down Margaret, just take a breath and calm down,' she said to herself. 'There must be an explanation.'

'George?' she shouted, her voice quivering slightly. 'George?' she shouted again louder.

No answer.

She cursed her grating bones as she eased herself gently from the bed and pulled on her dressing gown and slippers. She placed a hand on the bed to steady herself and made her way into the bathroom. Her eye was immediately drawn to the sink. There was only one toothbrush. A deep wrenching in her gut forced her to sit down on the toilet seat. A million thoughts span randomly through her head but she only caught one repeating 'he's left you Margaret, he's left you'. She sat for a minute rocking slowly back and forth holding her head in her hands, as if she could prevent the reality of what was in her head from spilling out into the world.

'Think, Margaret, think … what happened? Did we argue? What did we do yesterday?'

But she could not remember. Everything seemed so foggy. In a trance she made her way to the phone, at least that was still where it was supposed to be, and dialled the first number that came into her head.

'Dan, Daniel is that you?' she asked

'Yes Mum, where are you? You were meant to be here half an hour ago. You're late. We need to get to the church.'

'The church?' she repeated.

'Yes Mum – the christening, the ...'

She interrupted mid-sentence 'What? What are you talking about ... Dan I need to tell you, well it's important. I ...' and her voice faltered

'What Mum? What's wrong?'

'Your Dad. I think, I think he's left me.'

She paused waiting for his reaction, any reaction, but all she heard was a muffled 'it's happened again, Alison', accompanied by a deep sigh at the other end.

'What's happened again Dan?' she said, her voice cracking.

'Mum, don't you remember?'

Silence.

'Remember?' she repeated.

'Yes – don't you remember, what, what ...' His voice dropped to a barely audible whisper, 'what happened to Dad?'

'What do you mean, what happened to Dad?'

'Dad's gone, Mum.'

'Well, I know that – I told you...'

'No, I mean Dad's gone ... Listen I'll come round now, right now ... just wait a minute or two.'

He heard a thump and then nothing.

The phone swung loosely from its cord, while she remained motionless on the landing. It was coming back to her now – that phone call, the voice that said 'We're really very sorry to have to tell you, Mrs Clitheroe.' The tears, the funeral – it all came hurtling back through the tunnel of her mind with such force it took her breath away. How could she forget? She never could.

'I'll have to go over there, Alison. I can't leave her when she's like this.'

'But Dan, it's our child's christening for God's sake. She'll be fine, she always is.'

'No, I have to go. Have some bloody sympathy, will you? She's my Mum.' And with that Dan screeched out of the driveway and down the road.

He let himself in as usual. The house was silent apart from

a soft whimpering sound that came from the top of the stairs.

'Mum?'

He spied her crouched on the landing, hugging a white shirt to her chest. 'Mum,' he whispered, gently prising the cloth from her fingers. 'Mum … it's OK,' and held her cocooned in his arms while she wept. Her fragile frame shook violently with each sob. They stayed like this for some time until she lifted her face to him and said: 'I think your Dad's having an affair, there's lipstick on his shirt.'

Shauna Leishman

THEODORA'S THINKING THROUGH

'The calm before the storm,' whispered across Theodora's mind as she trudged across the heath. You know, I haven't actually seen that here in England, she thought, in response. Not like those times in The States where the air, the sky, sound, everything stops as if holding its breath. The scariest times are when the sky has a yellowish tinge, almost like a sickly moss around the edge – tornado weather, that is. Or the thunder and lightning, so exciting, but she hadn't seen much of that here either. She loved that still point, with a looming black sky, before the first CRACK which always made the bones jump, followed by the gusts, the rain, booming flashes from the sky, which beat any human-made entertainment for sheer excitement.

That one summer she spent in Oklahoma, while in high school, had been the best for thunderstorms. She'd sat on the porch, looking out over the plains and just watched thunderstorms rolling across, one after another. Week after week. She hated that place. Provincial, small-minded didn't begin to describe it. The town drove out all black people just fifteen years before and were still proud enough of that feat, to have a boast of it reach her ears. She'd survived the muggy, dripping, hot summer which sapped her mind and body of any thought or ambition, mourning the move from the beloved Arizona mountains, by steadily reading her way through the entire Barbara Cartland series found at the local library. The year before, she'd conquered snowdrifts to consume *The Lord of the Rings*. How far doth we fall. Theodora laughed bitterly. Since that Oklahoma summer, she'd never been able to even finish a page of a Barbara Cartland, it being so dull. Funny how authors of such diverse books had both been English.

And now here she is, trudging across, dare she say it? –

Heathcliff country.

Maybe she'll finally meet her Heathcliff – and hopefully have an encounter as one always found the last few pages of a Barbara – 'I … thought … you hated … me… I …' passionate kiss, smoldering eyes, wide shoulders, heaving bosom, elegant dress being torn, ' … love …' The women were always petite too, damn it.

Yeah, right, like that's ever going to happen. 'What is that up ahead? Why aren't there any of those glorious oaks around here?' Theodora muttered. That's one of the things she loved in England, not this, this bleak landscape, although the sky did liven it up. There is no calm here, nor any predictability, the sun constantly plays games with the clouds and you never know who is going to win any round.

Theodora headed, hopefully, towards an adventure. She had jumped in the car that morning and started driving. She liked to pick a direction and head that way until something looked intriguing and she could pull over. She never could do this in The States; it's just not in the design for her to do it there. She's always had the impulses – her mother still hasn't forgiven her for the way she'd run off at age two – but then that leash her mother finally found, began to limit her options.

Theodora knows she can't actually run away for good. She always goes back and things are the same and she has to push through it but the runs are her respites. Now that she has some freedom, money, transport, she can run with the wind if she needs, or sometimes, sit at the bottom of a cave as she'd done before. She'll soak in the elements, which never hurt her the way everything else can.

Except no, that's not exactly true – what about Yellowstone Park? Funny, these fields she was climbing through, empty of any of the type of beauty which is found in Yellowstone, are so much more invigorating. She doesn't feel the drain and even the utter horror that crept over her while she'd wander through steaming streams and black holes. Or even snowmobiling through the woods and fields that one time. Snow, yes, she hadn't missed snow either, so bleak and quiet and white and cold and deadly. Yes, give me these black clouds, shot through with rays of sun, constantly changing, fascinating, she thinks, thankful to be right here for the moment.

She pondered the Yellowstone phenomena again. She hadn't been there for years now, but back when she discovered her reaction to it she wondered long and hard. Had it been a place of tremendous wars at one time? Had she been brutally murdered there in another life? Is there an inherent evil in the sulphur pits? She'll never know. And now, she actually lives on a road called Wargraves (only in England, she smiles) and doesn't feel the dread she did in Yellowstone.

Thinking about this diverts her from her current problems, especially because it literally is on the other side of the world and far in the past. Or is it? Why has Yellowstone popped up on her register again? Several people have mentioned it recently and then she'd just read about it in Bryson's science book. Apparently, it has been discovered to be probably the largest volcano in the world – and it is active.

'That wouldn't happen here,' she says as she stops and looks back to see how far she'd come by now. Then turns again to wonder how far she is supposed to go this time. To the horizon or beyond? Wherever she finds herself on these adventures is always perfect. England is perfect – yes, it has some wicked windstorms – or relentless grey days, but never like that winter in Utah where she didn't see the mountain she lived under for two months. No inversions here, she thinks. Oh, and the ground doesn't shake much, at least never that mind-numbing, bone-freezing, life-shattering terror a big earthquake causes.

Theodora watches the sun illuminate a path ahead of her for a moment, glistening, and the dull plants suddenly brilliantly multicoloured. She feels herself expanding, her stresses flying off her like they can no longer get a grip. She twirls for a minute; she can do anything she wants here in this wild, empty space. It's full of energy and life and even beauty where the dreariness and radiance interplay like it wouldn't, if the day had a bland, blue sky, void of clouds. 'But that's a rare day in England, thank goodness,' Theodora says aloud.

What are not rare, she thinks, are these crazy people I have in my life. And I can't have just one – it has to be three, along with my oblivious husband. There will be no help from that quarter but that woman is not getting him anyway. Her two English friends, Kelly and then Frank, brought true meaning to the phrase 'with friends like these, who needs enemies?'

Theodora had just discovered Kelly, who has clung to her as a friend, is avidly chasing her husband behind her back. How could someone be so attentive and friendly, act like you are their best friend, look you in the eye, telling you about how much you've helped her and how wonderful you are, while at the same time sending suggestive emails and texts to your husband? Why does she even have his numbers and address? Why didn't he say anything for a couple of months? Theodora can excuse him, he's clueless and thinks she is just being friendly but Kelly is wily. Her husband had finally gotten nervous, confessed all and is now forwarding Kelly's messages to Theodora for her to deal with it. Theodora doesn't know what to do yet. Kelly has a husband, four kids and just wants to throw her own mess away and take over Theodora's life. Wasn't there a creepy movie once made about just such a thing?

As if that weren't enough, she also had her sister. After listening for years to her moaning about her husband, Theodora had suggested that she had to get approval from sisters, before getting involved with anyone again. Betty had eagerly agreed. Her divorce was finalised and she walked out of the courtroom doors to throw herself into Frank's arms, waiting on the stairs for her, a stranger just arrived for a visit from England. Theodora knew him to be a jerk under his charm. She had counselled with him around some of those issues and the plan had been to only stay with her family for a couple of weeks. But of course, Frank, eager to find a way to stay in the US, is going to be wooing a potential wife, even though he would become a vicious philanderer as soon as he had her. Theodora's whole family is watching in shock as a new drama begins and nobody can get through to Betty, again, and Theodora is getting the blame for having dumped Frank on them in the first place.

'Boundaries,' she mutters. All these people have serious boundary issues. Kind of like this landscape where there are no boundaries to be seen. While this is great for a wander, it can be problematic with people.

A little voice whispers, 'You are on the high ground here.' Theodora glances around and notices she has reached the top of a rise and she can see for miles, all sloping away from her. The scrawny tree she has been heading towards is right behind her.

Her mind is calm, she's breathing deeply, her body is invigorated, she's felt the quiet reassurances that this too shall pass and she would be okay.

As she turns to head back to her car, it begins to rain. That's okay too. Theodora grins and breaks into a slow jog. As she always tells her kids: 'Don't worry, you'll dry.'

Nemma Wollenfang

ENDLESS NUPTIALS

People were now saying that the wedding was cancelled. Kiera, the maid of honour, could hear them whispering it in the aisles, all the way to the back by the main doors. And she could see their point ... even if she would not concede it.

'No, no, everything is fine,' she told the guests, ushering an elderly couple back to their seats. 'It is all being sorted out as we speak.'

The florist had failed to show up and the caterers were late. One of the bridesmaids had gone into labour (but she was overdue anyway), the harpist was drunk, the flower girl was squalling, and the best man had broken his little toe. But really... was that reason enough to cancel? Surely it was still salvageable.

'It's eleven o'five,' the groom's uncle, Mr Henderson, complained, tapping his watch.

'I know,' Kiera said patiently. 'I'm sure it will start shortly.'

'But it's eleven o'five,' he persisted. 'It was supposed to start at ten fifty.'

Kiera only smiled as she walked along. What else could she say? And besides, they were only running a few minutes late...

Niamh, her best friend since toddler group, was the bride-to-be, and this was her 'Big Day' with a capital B. It was something she had dreamt about since childhood. Niamh had sat Kiera through Barbie and Ken ceremonies when they were five, set up that wedding with Bobby Marks (and made her preside over it) when they were in year three, and at every opportunity since she had become engaged to Chris two years ago she had dragged Kiera to any wedding fair she could find with a smile and a giggle. This meant a lot to Niamh, and Kiera was going to make sure it happened for her.

'How are you doing, Bee?' Kiera asked as she approached

the labouring bridesmaid in the back row. A flock of women surrounded her, fretting and fussing. Her cheeks were red, her brow dappled with sweat, and she was taking quick breaths as she nodded.

'Good,' she gasped, 'good-good. Don't worry about me.'

She waved Kiera away. It seemed wrong to leave her, even with her retinue, and Kiera would have stayed had she not noticed the woman in khakis hefting a bundle of flowers through the church doors. Ah, the florist! But…

'Oh no!' Kiera gasped. 'These are orange lilies. We specifically said white roses!'

'Sorry,' the florist said as she deposited her load, 'but my form here says otherwise. The Lawson-Fowler wedding, right?'

'No, this is the Blakely-O'Connor wedding.'

'Ah,' the florist said awkwardly. 'Perhaps you can just use these. I'll knock half off the price and besides, it's a little late to change them now.'

Kiera sighed dejectedly. 'But Niamh hates orange lilies…'

There was nothing else to be done though, and at a wedding there had to be some flowers. So she allowed the florist and her two-man team to set them up.

As she made her way back up the aisle, she bypassed the inebriated harpist, strumming a slow and horribly disorderly tune.

'Err, perhaps something a little softer,' she said as kindly as she could.

The man gave her a waving thumbs-up and what could have been a 'Sure thing, sweetie' but with the way he fumbled the words it was difficult to tell.

Another squeal punctuated the air and Kiera cringed as she passed the flower girl, red-faced in her mother's lap. Her mother could only look at Kiera sadly and mouth 'toothing'.

In a chamber at the back of the church, Kiera found a small kitchen – a communal room for church staff – complete with fridge and freezer, and after a brief investigation she found what she wanted and headed to the front pews and the best man.

'An ice-pack for your toe,' she said. 'Perhaps it will help with the swelling.'

He thanked her and, with a wince, set it firmly to his foot.

Things were getting sorted, Kiera assured herself as she looked about. The flowers made the church a little brighter, the pregnant bridesmaid appeared to be calming, and the best man was carefully testing his toe and managing to stand. Slowly, all was falling into place. This could still happen. Kiera was sure.

Up at the altar, Chris, the dashing young groom, was a nervous wreck.

'I should call the whole thing off,' he muttered as he paced. 'The day is ruined.'

'Not yet,' Kiera said as she approached. 'The ceremony can still be saved.'

Chris did not look so certain; his brow puckered into a grimace. 'Look around you,' he said, gesturing to the room at large – to the slurring harpist, the orange lilies, the squealing child and the disgruntled guests… 'There was more civility in Sodom and Gomorrah. It's a disaster!'

As if to emphasis his distress, Mr Henderson called from his place in the aisles. 'It's eleven twenty.'

The clock was ticking – as if they needed reminding. The bride would be here soon. And Kiera was getting a headache.

'All that's needed is a little authority,' she assured. 'Someone to calm the rabble and quell the disorder.'

His disbelieving stare held a hint of hope. 'And you can do that?'

'If Niamh does not find out beforehand, I can.' She hoped. Her best friend's wedding depended on it.

The vicar approached. 'May I be of some assistance?'

He was surprisingly young for a 'man of the cloth', in his early thirties, with film-star dark hair that swished and a charming smile that made even the matronly parishioners swoon.

Could vicars marry? Kiera wondered. Not the point! There was a wedding to save.

Chris turned to him with gratitude. 'Oh, Father. Thank God!'

'Appropriate words,' the vicar said wryly.

'We could use your help, yes.' Suddenly enthused, Chris took his arm and steered him aside. 'My beloved bride will soon be stepping into this church and I cannot have her seeing the assembly in this…' he struggled for the word, 'state. Perhaps if someone were to go and comfort her before the ceremony, provide a kind word or two, tell her that everything is fine?' His entreaty held a suggestive lilt.

The vicar frowned. 'Lying is a grievous sin.'

'Hmm, where do you stand on truth abbreviation?'

Leaving the men to their talk, Kiera set about conducting more of her own damage control. She checked on the ambulance (on its way), conjured a lollipop for the crying child, and brought a healthy dose of spring-water for the harpist, while the vicar set off to 'distract' the bride.

'It's eleven thirty,' Mr Henderson persisted as she passed.

Behind him, a number of guests subtly tried to vacate their seats, their eyes on the exit.

'Just a few more minutes, please,' Kiera practically begged, leading the wandering guests back to their places. 'The ceremony will be underway shortly.'

Eventually, with a little prompting, the bedlam quieted down. The crowning bridesmaid was carted away by hasty EMT's. The harpist sobered enough to pluck a subtle melody. The flower girl sat quiescent in her mother's lap sucking her treat, and the best man limped to the altar with a pained smile and a big thumbs-up.

Salvageable, Kiera reminded herself, it was still salvageable.

Niamh would get her special day.

Ten minutes and two aspirin later, they were all set to go and only awaiting the bride, when the last remaining bridesmaid came wandering up the aisle. Her steps faltered and her face was pale.

Oh no, what now? Sensing it was nothing good, Kiera swiftly ushered her to a quiet corner – away from wagging ears.

'What's wrong?' she asked, as quietly as she could.

'It's the bride,' the bridesmaid said. 'She's run off with the vicar!'

No, it was definitely not salvageable.

Previously published in Ourtown Magazine

Marian Smith

CONCRETE AND CONSEQUENCES

'My dear Mr Wickham, do you really think Mr and Mrs Darcy would be offended by our arriving without an invitation?'

'Not at all my dear Lizzie, I am sure they would welcome it as a pleasant diversion in their lives.'

Elizabeth Wickham was not convinced by her husband's assertions but smiled and nodded in agreement.

When they arrived at Pemberley they were surprised to see Darcy appear from the garden in only breeches and shirt, covered in dust and perspiring heavily.

'My dear Darcy,' said Wickham, 'do explain yourself!'

Darcy looked flustered and not at all pleased to see them, but he forced a smile. 'Wickham, Elizabeth, how delightful to see you. You must excuse my appearance – I have given Wiggins the gardener a few days off and as I felt bored with hunting and going to balls and playing cards, I resolved to build a new terrace behind the house.'

'Really?' they both said in unison. 'What a singularly strange thing to do.'

Darcy took them to the garden where they surveyed a large hole filled with a thick grey slimy matter.

'Excellent my dear Darcy, but you do look rather dusty,' observed Wickham.

'That would be the concrete,' declared Darcy, 'If only there was a machine to mix it. Such a device has not been invented, but I have managed to dig a very sizeable hole and fill it with the concrete and I am most satisfied with the result.'

Lizzie then ventured to ask: 'And what does Lydia think of this endeavour?'

Darcy looked most agitated at this question but recovered himself. 'Mrs Darcy has gone up to town.'

'She has?' said Lizzie, most surprised. 'She said nothing to me of such a plan. When will she be back?'

Darcy glanced at the new terrace and Lizzie was sure that he give a brief smile.

'I do declare,' he said, 'she may be some time...'

Bill Webster

RAFFLES-BROWN GOES TO TOWN

'Ah! Pensions Day!'

Raffles-Brown threw off the bedcovers and walked naked to the en-suite, pausing in front of the full-length mirror to check himself out from various angles.

'Bloody amazing for seventy-eight! Who would have believed it?' He continued to the bathroom, with a sigh and a little shake of his head. 'Too bad you didn't live to see it, Poppy, old girl.'

Shaving was accomplished in a few deft strokes of a venerable and vicious cut-throat razor, before the state-of-the-art power shower sluiced away the final remnants of sleep.

Ablutions done, he pulled on a pair of baggy shorts and wandered out into the early morning sunshine with an antique samurai sword.

A husky cultivated voice broke into the introspection of his tai-chi routine. 'Good morning Raffles-Brown! It's a lovely start to the day, don't you think?'

'And all the lovelier for seeing you, Mrs Whitely!'

'How many times do I have to tell you to call me Susan?'

He laughed. 'And how many times do I have to tell you that that would not do at all, Mrs Whitely! Especially when you wear that black bikini! No indeed! Thinking of you as 'Mrs Whitely' helps to remind this old man that he's almost old enough to be your grandfather!'

She brushed her auburn hair back from her tanned face and surveyed the sky. 'Looks like it's going to be a hot one, Mr Raffles-Brown. Maybe the black bikini will be coming out this afternoon.' She smiled.

'In that event it will be a most auspicious day indeed, Mrs Whitely. In fact it has been a most pleasant six months since you took the let on the Garden Cottage. How's that thriller of yours coming on, anyway?'

'I'm on the second draft now, but my editor has raised some questions about authenticity so I'm into a second research phase now.' She grinned disarmingly. 'Rather exciting in fact, and I must get back to it now.'

Raffles-Brown's keen nose caught the distinctive leather fragrance of her perfume as she headed back towards the cottage.

Exercise finished he returned to the house, brushed his full grey hair, and dressed in tweed plus-fours with a matching shooting jacket set off by one of his favourite mustard yellow cravats. He trimmed a couple of wayward hairs from his moustache, and then it was time to break his fast.

His housekeeper had his regulation poached eggs on toast ready for him as he entered the spacious dining kitchen with its view down to the walled gardens beyond the manicured lawns.

'Good morning, my dear Mrs McHardy, and how are you today?'

'Same as ever, Mr Raffles-Brown. I have womanly things that never seem to be quite right, really.'

Raffles-Brown harrumphed sympathetically in reply and poured himself precisely three quarters of a cup of lapsang-souchong which he then topped up with a shot of Laphroaig from his hip flask.

He smacked his lips. 'Ah! That first cup of tea of the day! Always so very refreshing!'

Breakfast done, he left Mrs McHardy gloomily going about her duties, topped up his hip flask, picked up his cane, and set off for the village. He walked briskly down the avenue to the main gate, the metal tip of his cane tapping out the beat of his progress.

Five minutes later he turned out the gate onto the road that would take him to the village. It was less than a mile from here to the post office, but the walk generally took an extended time as Raffles-Brown passed the time of day with those he met along the way.

Today was no different. As he approached the crossroads

just outside the village he heard noises of human exertion and straining mechanicals behind him. Brakes squealed as the village bobby gratefully pulled up for a chat. 'What ho, Mr Raffles-Brown!'

'Sergeant Arthur! How splendid to see you! But you must take it easier on that machine of yours. It's not the *Tour de France*, you know!' Raffles-Brown fished into an inside pocket and presented the Laphroaig to the rotund and red-faced policeman.

Sergeant Arthur took a quick look round, and then took the proffered hip flask. 'Thank you, sir. I must record that I am on duty at this time, but this is for medicinal purposes only, you understand.' He tipped the flask to his lips.

'Quite, quite, Sergeant Arthur.' Raffles-Brown retrieved the flask and had a quick stiffener himself before pocketing it again.

'So, what's happening in the world of law enforcement today, Sergeant?'

'Nothing much so far.' He paused. 'In fact, nothing at all if the truth be told. I think my zero-tolerance policy must be paying off. And what about you, sir? Off to the post office, are we?'

'Yes, indeed I am! You know me too well,' he chuckled. 'I don't even need the bally-silly pension, but it's a great day for seeing people and dropping in for a couple of pints and a bite to eat at The Dog.'

'You bloody pensioners! Life of Riley! I hope I live long enough to join in the party!' His brow suddenly furrowed. 'Oh! Talking of pensioners reminds me. If it hadn't been for me being near death's door before I took that excellent medicine of yours, I would have said earlier. It may be quiet on my patch, Raffles-Brown, but did you hear about the spot of excitement they had over at Tidcaster the other day?'

Raffles-Brown indicated with a slight shake of his head that he had not.

'Well, some young hooligan rode in on a motorbike and held the post office up at gunpoint, no less!'

'No! At gunpoint you say? Surely not round these parts!'

'I'm afraid so, Mr Raffles-Brown. Pulled a pistol out of his jacket as calm as you like and told Ted Hollings the postmaster to hand over the effing money or he'd blow his effing head off, pardon my French.'

'The little scamp!' Raffles-Brown exclaimed.

'So anyway, we've all been told to keep a lookout for this fellow in case he tries it on again. Slim build, about five foot-seven, black helmet, black leathers, and a dark visor.'

'Well, that ties it down!' Raffles-Brown said with a sympathetic smile. 'Anything else apart from the fact that he has a foul mouth on him? The make of the motorcycle maybe?'

'We're not absolutely sure on that, but it's a big bike... maybe a Honda. Oh, and despite the foul mouth, old Mrs Thomas was most insistent that it was someone with a posh accent trying to disguise their voice.'

'OK Sergeant, I'll keep my eyes open and let you know if I see anything suspicious.'

'Thank you for that, Mr Raffles-Brown.' He checked his bicycle clips and remounted his machine. As he wobbled off towards the village he turned and waved. 'And thanks for the medicine, too!'

Raffles-Brown smiled and continued on his way, the tip of the cane tapping out its regular beat.

It was only about five minutes later that the big Honda purred past. Black helmet, black visor, black leathers.

Raffles-Brown quickened his pace. He strode past the Dog & Partridge and turned into the main street.

There was the post office, and right outside was the Honda on its stand with its engine idling lumpily.

'This is a right rum to-do,' he murmured as he surveyed the scene. Then he smiled as his sensitive nose picked up the lingering scent in the air.

The post office door opened and the motorcyclist came out, stuffing a black polythene bin bag down the front of the partially-zipped black jacket ... but then stopped stock still at the sight of the old man astride the bike.

Raffles-Brown found himself looking down the wrong end of a pistol.

'Gerroff that fucking bike now, mate, or you're dead!'

The old man searched for the eyes behind the visor. He could not see them but knew the impact his steady gaze would have. He laughed cheerily. 'If I get off this bike now, it'll fall. I don't think either of us have the strength to lift it, and you're running out of time.'

The gun trembled in the motorcyclist's weak two-handed grip.

That keen nose twitched and twitched again. Raffles-Brown's smile assumed gigantic proportions.

'Put that toy gun away. And get on the bike now because I think I feel an angina attack coming on! Research my arse!'

As the bike roared away, Sergeant Arthur approached at full speed and skidded to a halt, the bicycle sliding out from underneath him and depositing him in a heap beside the prostrate Raffles-Brown. 'Have you been shot, sir? Oh please God, don't let him have been shot!'

Raffles-Brown's hand appeared from under his body clutching the hip flask. He sat up ruefully and took a deep draft of Laphroaig, before offering it to the winded Sergeant Arthur.

'In my day, Sergeant Arthur, I would have apprehended the villain, but I suppose age comes to all of us.'

He sat in the road, with Sergeant Arthur's perspiring head in his lap, drinking Laphroaig, and wondering if a day would ever come when the female of the species would finally hold no more surprises for him.

Tom Ireland

MAKING CONTACT

For eighty years, a blurred world, edges smeared,
faces simply lumps of uncooked pastry.
Stupid at school, the board unseen,
till glasses cleared the images,
installed edges, clear clean lines, distinctions.
So specky four-eyes, goggle-face, professor … I feigned
deafness, a comforting protective habit.
Blank looks, puzzled frowns turneth away wrath. Mostly.
Years creep by; eyes grow bedazzled, stars grow halos,
car headlights radiate a thousand suns, a match
flares like a launched rocket headed for the moon.
Colours cascade, cataracting insanely, defying gravity.
'Perhaps it's time to consider action,' a white-coated voice
suggests, flooding my eyes with torchlight.
I clasp straws and nod.
Scrutinised, tested, artificial tears, diamond-bright searching,
And knowing there is a knife hovering;
simply a thrust, no sense of sharpness, painless.
A deluge of shivering water floods my eye,
detritus of the faulty lens washes away.
A thrust installs the superior man-made lens.
Six minutes' discomfort; then a legislation of instruction,
driven home through an even brighter blaze of lights.
Fearing that this has all been in vain and vanity,
a restless sleep. Eventually, the eyepatch discarded,
a new world rushes into view. Bird-table-focused
blackbirds flaunt their glowing feathers,
wintering trees demonstrate their tiniest twig,
and a boy, three rows in front of me on the bus,
texts his longing to his reluctant mate.
Night-time shadows threaten sleep.

I, plotting and planning in my warm bed,
can clearly see the monsters.

Liz Leech

A WALK AT MIDNIGHT

The night was cold, with a stiff breeze that sent wispy clouds scudding across the face of a near full moon.

Will guessed that there would be flying tonight, all the more reason to be annoyed with Frank. They had set off in good time up the hill leading towards the town and the concrete radio transmission station where they were due to relieve the present crew at 12am. Will liked to look smart, think sharp and be on time. It was partly for these attributes that he had been posted here to the flat lands of Bedfordshire. Another reason was that he had above average night vision. He paused, not for the first time, wondering how on earth Frank had slipped through the net. A likeable man for all that, but where was he? It didn't take this long to go back and collect his missing kit.

Will did a three hundred and sixty degree turn, surveying the land spread out before him, ever the farmer, looking for the potential, or in this case how land might be managed had it not been requisitioned by the Airforce and buried under several hundred tons of concrete runway, but this airfield was special. He had learned since his arrival two months ago, that you kept your eyes open, noticed nothing and said even less. No new arrival got past the gates without being marched into an office to sign the Official Secrets Act. You did not ask questions, and more importantly you did not talk unless you were very sure that you knew who you were talking to.

All the more reason for Will to start, when someone called out, 'George, well bless me, what brings you to these parts?'

Will spun round, instantly on the alert. To his surprise, bright moonlight revealed an old man leaning against a gate post. A jovial voice in a melancholy face was the first impression. A countryman of casual appearance, bewhiskered and wearing a deep-pocketed coat of indeterminate age who seemed at home in his surroundings.

'It is George isn't it, by Jove,' the man said, pushing himself away from the gate and moving forward his arms swinging ready for a familiar greeting. He paused, lack of recognition having him confused. 'You're not George?'

'No, I'm not your George.'

'Bye lad, you're the spitting image of him, even sound the same. Is this some prank?'

'Just what I was wondering. What brings you here at this time of night? Who are you?'

'Jervaise Dance, known well in these parts. Ask anyone. I thought that I would come back,' the man said wistfully, 'and just take a look at the place. I lived here at Waterford Farm and afore that at Longford End for nigh on forty years. I loved every inch of this ground – not everybody's choice, hard work with the clay and it being so damp, especially in winter. It takes a special sort of knowledge, and I had it, but they cast me out. A change of ownership, stupid lawyers from London, didn't know a thing, talked of consolidating and making bigger profits. The place went down hill fast after that, and broke the hearts of several stout men.'

Will nodded, his mind flashed back to Kenya's red soil, the sounds and smell of the fast onset of evening, the sun briefly silhouetting row upon row of freshly weeded coffee bushes before it sunk in a moment. He had never tired of those sudden African sunsets, but the financial slump put paid to that dream; he had come home and moved on. Then it had happened again, with his having to relinquish his tenancy of Battern Farm after he volunteered to become an airman.

Will dragged himself back to the present. 'We must be moving,' he said, thinking quickly. It would be best to get this extraordinary man up the hill and away from the hub of activity down below. Why was he here and how had he got past all the barriers and who, after all, was George?

'Right you are, lad. I could do with a stroll, and the view is a way better from up there.' He turned to look around as he spoke and then let out an audible gasp. 'What have they done with Allan's elms? Oh, he would not be pleased with that sight – no, he would not.'

Will followed his gaze to where until recently, a clump of majestic elms had topped the ridge above Warden Park. Sadly planes needed to take off and land safely, with not much room to manoeuvre. The trees had to go. Will hurriedly turned him away.

'He loved those trees – planted them himself,' muttered Jervaise, pulling a handkerchief out of his breeches pocket and mopping his forehead as if to wipe away the vision. 'He lived at Warden Park. It was good to have my eldest son so close. He was fond of cricket and used to hold matches there. Do you enjoy a game of cricket?' He paused. 'I'm sorry – what's your name?'

'Will.'

'Will, now would that be a shortening of William or Wilfred? As I recall George called his eldest son Wilfred. Your father is not called George by any chance?'

'No, I come from a long line of Wilfreds. At least, it is my fathers name and his before him. My wife is pregnant with our second, if it's a boy, he'll be another Wilfred. I was discussing it with the missus on my last leave.'

'I had sons – the third was called after me. My wife took this strange notion of calling the first two after family names – her family mind. You have to humour women, but I am blessed if I know how they cope with such handles.'

'I have my mother's surname as a middle name, keeps a link to her family I suppose.'

'Yes, but in our case, it was not only family names she was giving them, but places as well. My wife grew up in Mardon, not far from Biggleswade and now I have a son and two grandsons named after the place!' The same went on in Martha's family. Daft lot of women if you ask me, but they wouldn't be turned on the question of naming their sons. They were close those two: my Jane being the eldest and Martha the baby by fifteen years.'

'Martha.' Will ran the name across his tongue like a distant memory.

'Martha was George's wife,' said Jervaise. 'Her father upped sticks when she was still a child – went south. She ended up marrying a farmer from Wiltshire. I would guess you are of farming stock. What's your line boy?'

'Mixed farming generally but dairy in particular. I'm building up a herd of Guernseys. And you?'

'Market gardening is the thing around here, lad. Peas and beans and such like. I'm quite pleased with the importation of Scottish seed potatoes, but the blight is a trial to us in these low lying fields. If I had a partiality, it would be for beans and horses.'

'Now you're talking. That's something I miss over here – horses, and hunting.'

'You cannot beat a good race across a field when your blood's up, can you, lad?'

At that moment he tripped and stumbled on the path, and the other lent a hand to help him right himself. Jervaise was for looking down the hill again, but he was deftly turned around. It was a moon-night after all.

'Someone needs to sort this path out,' he said by way of an excuse. 'Hedges need to be grubbed out too. Why, I had a broody hen, used to always creep off and lay a clutch of eggs under this here hedge, if I didn't keep it clean and no matter how hard one looked, she was never found until she decided to present herself with a string of chicks in her wake. The fox never had her, though it would take a couple from the barn every year. Broody hens, who would have them, always pick the wrong time or the wrong place. Women you see, nothing but a blathering nuisance the lot of them,' but he said it with an inflection in his voice which told another story.

Will tensed, on his guard again. Was this man playing tricks with him? One minute he seemed like just a slightly daft old farmer and then the next … like a plant from the Hun!' He didn't look like a spy, but who knows? Whatever he was, *broody hen* was not something to say lightly around here. Logic would say that here was a farmer, and what farmer didn't keep chickens? But *broody hen* was also the code name for a directional device that they had been testing right here along with another called *oboe* that would go towards improving bombing accuracy, not to mention saving the lives of many returning airmen. It was too important a device to fall into the hands of the enemy.

Will took another glance at Jervaise and then threw him a broadside. 'Is there anyone musical in your family, who might play a wind instrument?'

'Don't be daft,' came the rapid reply. 'What use have we for the likes of such fripperies. There is not much space in a farmers life for playing the flute or what not, bah', he said with disgust.

Will was somewhat relieved. He wanted to be at the bunker set up and ready to go, when the transmissions started. See them out and see them back in on one watch. There was talk of smaller planes coming to the station, but for now it was testing, testing, testing with big lumbering Wellingtons – not ideal for this field, but what a plane!

As if on cue, a quiet rumble erupted down below them.

'What is that? Oh, my Lord, what is happening?' moaned Jervaise.

The volume was cranking up and a lumbering giant crept towards them on the hill. Jervaise dived for cover. Will turned, he couldn't help but watch as the plane lifted above the ground, working hard to gain height to clear the hill, moonlight giving a thin line of definition to its dark bulk, and then it was gone, away into the distance.

Will lent down for a second time to help the elderly man to his feet. He read shock and wide-eyed horror on the man's face, lit up like a ghost in the moonlight.

'Will, are you there? Sorry old chap, the guard kept me back, a lot of fuss that I had left you alone up here. It is so petty, having to go two by two like in the ark, what's a few hundred yards between pals on an airfield as secure as this one!'

'We're here,' let slip Will.

'We?'

As they climbed the hill, Will recollected that his grandfather who had died before he was born had lots of brothers, two had died in their thirties, one as a child, Allan ... he paused in astonishment, had gone to Australia and then there was lovely Uncle Philip and Ralf and ... Arthur Mardon, the baker who died when Will was seven.

'Well I'll be damned, he thought, taking a brief glance to left and right, but there was nothing: noone. He scratched his head and repositioning his forage cap called, 'Come on Frank, let's get on. There is going to be hell to play with us being late.'

Joyce Ireland

SEARCHING ARCHIVES

Family history's all the rage.
People queue to read the files
and crowd the Search Room for an age.
The archive soon will yield the dates.
Writings written so long ago.

The microfilm has much to show;
the microfiche is hard to read.
Computer records are so slow
to build the trees of family
from those writings long ago.

Uncle Joe ran off to sea;
Auntie Ruth was married once.
We have cousins yet to be
found in here, or somewhere else
in other writings long ago?

Clara Jane was Mum to Ken,
but what year did she marry Stan?
We know the where but not the when.
The Census doesn't help with that
in written lines so long ago.

Was Queen Victoria on the throne
when Herbert married Great Aunt Maud?
Is Fred the one who so loved Joan?
Why can't I find my Grandma's mum
with writings from so long ago?

Who was Daddy's Uncle Bill?
Why did he not inherit when
Great Grandpa was drawing up his will?
Do we have our own black sheep
shown in those writings long ago?

The ghosts come in and linger here;
they hold the secrets we would find.
Is this John Smith the one so dear
and was his house in Albert Road,
on maps drawn up so long ago?

The archivist is good with dates;
she knows the history of this town.
The records all are kept in crates
and files of pink or dusty fawn.
Stored and catalogued long ago.

Joan Carter

CHERRIES

Malcolm sighed deeply with pleasure as he looked through the window to his back garden.

It was early. The lawn was still damp. He surveyed the garden with pride. It had never looked better. All his own work. All his own garden. Not overlooked. Well stocked with trees, flowers, fruit and vegetables. And mostly organic. He was practically self-sufficient. He believed in natural methods for removing the various weeds, moulds, mites, parasites, wasps, Cabbage White butterflies and other pests that were the bane of his summer life – spoiling his crops and reducing his impressive yields. And most of his methods worked well. Didn't he always have the best displays at the Flower and Produce Show and win most prizes? And that included the men's pie competition. He had won three years in a row with his gooseberry pie and was planning to surprise them this year with a new triumph – his giant pot-grown blueberries were doing so well.

Wasn't he glad to be single again? He could look after the garden every day of the week. He didn't have to spend pointless Saturday mornings shopping and Sundays taking Margaret to one or other of other people's gardens. What was the point of that? All he could ever see were the many faults that let those other gardens down.

That was Margaret's point too, he remembered, as she packed her bags to leave him.

'You always think you're best at everything Malcolm,' she said. 'Well, I've had enough. Nothing I do is good enough. I'm leaving you. And don't worry. I don't want anything from you, just my freedom. If we'd had children it might have been different. But of course you didn't want any in case they let you down. And you've become so mean. You even begrudge the birds a few of the cherries from the top of the tree.'

He hadn't wanted to tell people she'd left him. But in the end, he had to. He preferred to be honest. He told the few men in the Show committee that he knew best. They had seemed surprised but said nothing. Her few so-called friends took little interest in the news either. Neither he nor she had close family members to tell. Within weeks after she'd said goodbye he started living his life for himself. And that was that. That was two years ago. He had almost stopped missing her.

He found himself looking at the cherry tree. The tallest tree. Her favourite tree and the true glory of the garden. It had produced better than ever since he'd last seen her. Forty pounds of cherries last year. Could be more this year. Perhaps she would have been proud of it. A tear almost formed in his eye as he remembered the cherries she used to soak in Cognac for months then wrap in marzipan and dip in the best chocolate she could find before presenting him with them at Christmas. He didn't have the patience to do all that fiddling. Then he sniffed, stretched and contemplated his day. He realised he had not yet quite woken up. Was still a little tired. He'd have a good leisurely breakfast in his dressing gown. Then put on his gardening clothes for another day of pest removal. He glanced again at the tree.

Then: 'You bastards!' he spluttered.

As dark shapes shifted in the magnificent tree halfway up his garden, something dark shifted in Malcolm. His mind raced.

'You bloody birds! Right. That's it, you've had your last chance!' he spat out.

Malcolm hurried downstairs, to the back of the house and through the kitchen side door into his garage. He dragged the huge new plastic bottle down from a high shelf, a junior fretsaw from its outlined place on the wall and a black marker pen from the neat tub at the back of his wide workbench. He should have prepared this sooner!

Placing the sturdy container on the workbench, he leant his

body against it. As he had previously ascertained, it reached from his chin to his waist. He marked with a large dot the spot on the bottle opposite the centre of his breastbone. He carefully replaced the lid of the pen and laid the vessel on its back.

Undoing the pen again, Malcolm drew a line through the dot across the container, curved it up at the sides and into a diagonal up towards the back. Checking from side to side as he worked, he continued a vertical line to the top and just in front of the capped lid. Repeated this on the other side. He drew a large circle on the back. Capping the pen and replacing it in the tub, he checked his work. A swift nod of satisfaction and he started with the fretsaw, trying to take his time despite his desire to hurry.

Ten minutes later Malcolm was fitting the man-sized pelican bib he had created over his head. He looked down into the voluminous space and smiled that it weighed so little although it was so strong. A perfect receptacle for all the fruit. He was now prepared, as usual, for every eventuality.

The collar of his pyjamas protected his neck from the sharp edge of the cut plastic. He considered for a few seconds whether to line it with gaffer tape. No, it would be fine. This shouldn't take too long. He wasn't going to choose after all, he would pick them all. Every cherry.

Malcolm considered taking the time to change into his gardening clothes. No! He tied the belt of his dressing gown with a reef knot and thrust his feet into the wellingtons waiting at the back door from the garage into the garden. Nobody would see him, after all. Once again he was glad to have worked just that bit harder than other men, in order to be able to afford a detached house. No nosey neighbours looking in. He almost chuckled as he imagined somebody seeing him, dressed like this. A man in night clothes and a giant plastic bib. And for a fleeting second he imagined that he could be naked and nobody would know. For an even briefer time, he considered doing exactly that. But no, that would be ridiculous. And anyway, the plastic would then definitely be too sharp on his neck.

Malcolm strode over to the cherry tree, flapping his arms and causing, as he got nearer, a number of birds to flee in a panic. He noted they were several pigeons and a male blackbird.

'Bugger off you bastards,' he spat, not too loudly in case there may be a neighbour about. Though it was still so early he doubted it. He had never heard anyone about even at seven o'clock when he frequently started his weeding and even now on this fine July morning it was still only five thirty.

The ladder was propped into the tree. It was the only piece of garden equipment that Malcolm ever left out. He had tied it at the top and, being aluminium, it would not rust in any rain. He checked the rungs were dry enough and started a careful slow climb. Wellingtons weren't the best footwear. Perhaps he should go back and change? But no, he would be extra-careful. After all, it was only one climb up and one climb back. He was sure his patent cherry holder would hold every cherry. He smiled again at his cleverness, imagined himself telling them about it at the flower show.

At each rung he picked all the cherries he could reach and muttered, 'You greedy bloody bastards... You always get the cherries off the top of this tree. Aren't I allowed the rest? You have to break the rules don't you! I've tried everything to put you off. First it was old video tape. That lasted only one year. You ignored it the next. Then it was old CDs. Carefully suspended to spin and swing. Again a one-year wonder. Then the old washing-up gloves. They lasted two years, until now. And this old paper lampshade only worked for a while didn't it, with everything else still on the tree!'

Malcolm continued to pick cherries as he climbed and ranted. He negotiated his way up between the branches, dodging the gloves and tape and CDs that had lost their shine. He'd have to take them down later, they looked so untidy. At each step up he rested the cherry tub on a rung. After half an hour he had almost reached his usual stopping point and had to use both hands to lift the tub to its next resting spot. It was getting nicely full. What a very good idea!

At last he rested the base of the cherry collector on the top rung of the ladder and looked around him. Above his head he noticed there were still plenty of cherries.

'You bloody bastards!' he raged. 'You've been eating mine and left yours for last.'

As he looked, Malcolm saw that, true to form, like the blackberries on the railway brambles that were unreachable through train windows, these were the biggest and ripest cherries of all. Perfect. Perhaps even worth him going to the trouble of steeping in Cognac and all the rest of it. Those bloody birds would enjoy the very best of his cherries! He was so angry that for a second he imagined the steam that would come from his ears if he could manage such a trick. Then he realised it was not enough to be angry. He must do something.

A glance into the cherry holder showed him that it was only just over three quarters full. Plenty of space for more. He looked around and spotted a handy fork in the tree branches that would surely be wide enough for his foot.

He carefully took three more steps up the ladder. 'I'll show you bastards. If you're going to take mine. I'll have yours!'

There was only one rung above the one he was standing on, his other foot between the branches. He would never, ever, have taken the chance if he hadn't tied the ladder himself. He could feel that it was completely stable. He heaved the tub on to a branch for support, having to lean slightly forward to do so. He considered slipping his head from the plastic collar.

'No. Not a chance. I'll lose the lot if it falls.'

Holding on to the tree with one hand, he gingerly, then with more confidence, reached with his other hand for the fruit around him. It was so easy. The ripe cherries came off in huge plump clusters. He tasted one or two. Then a few more. Not like him to eat unwashed fruit, but they were so delicious that he could not resist. After just a few minutes the tub was almost full and his hand dripped to the elbow with sticky juice.

For a few seconds, looking at his streaked arm and pyjama sleeve, Malcolm was annoyed with himself. Then he smiled.

'It's all washable,' he said aloud.

This had been one of Margaret's sayings. Unaccountably, tears sprang into Malcolm's eyes. And he put up a hand to wipe them away. That was his first mistake. Wiping his eyes with fingers covered in cherry juice was his second. The pain caused him to flinch and straighten, and without thinking he let go of the tree.

Malcolm felt a heavy pain around his chest.

'My heart,' he thought. But it was not his heart. His third mistake, although of course really it had been his first, was to have made such a very large container for the cherries. As he shifted and the weight of the very many pounds and pounds of cherries left the branch and instead rested on Malcolm, his momentum changed.

Slowly, slowly, his chest toppled back. His feet left the ladder. He slid, back first, through the tree. The small twigs cut into his arms and face, his neck and head. The larger branches broke his fall. But they also broke one of his legs and both his arms. By the time he landed, Malcolm was in so much pain that he had passed out.

He came to, flat on his back. His face and shoulders were pinned to the ground by small red fruits. And pecking at the fruits were birds. Pigeons. Blackbirds. Sparrows.

Malcolm felt warm liquid filling his ears. It was his own tears. He could not move without enormous pain. Again he felt a pressure in his chest. This time it wasn't the weight of the cherries. It was his heart. He knew now that he had overdone it. Knew he would die here. It would probably be days before anyone missed him.

If only Margaret was here. She would have missed him, found him, called an ambulance.

'I'm sorry Margaret,' he sobbed. 'I'm so sorry.'

He turned his head to the side and whispered towards the earth. 'I'm so sorry Margaret. I should have let you go. But I couldn't. This was always your favourite tree, wasn't it. That's why I chose it. That's why I buried you here.'

Bill Webster

CLIMATE CHANGE

(A bad poem with good form.)

On every medium it's the news that is current
Climate change causes all ills, and makes it rain
But then I look to the sky and I see the sun
And cogitate on how its radiation can cause a hurricane
While astronomers tell us to beware of the sunspot
That triggers the change that'll cause the planet's death

There are many these days who believe that death
Will result from all the pollution that is current
Combined with mighty forces like the dreaded sunspot
That makes the most god-awful wind and rain
Surging and storming like a tropical hurricane
Blowing palms and cars and houses and blotting the sun

And yet every morning I awake to see the glorious sun,
Thus proving that my little land has avoided death!
Not for leafy Cheshire the wild tornado or hurricane
Bringing misery and leaving us without electric current,
But rather frost and snow and periods of rain
That may or may not be the result of a sunspot

And while we're on the subject, just what is a sunspot?
Some people might say that it is simply a spot on the sun
But these are the same people who watch *Singing in the Rain*
And believe it was filmed outside and thus deserve death
After which their bodies should be carried out to sea on a current
Which will ideally take them into the gaping maw of a hurricane

I don't think it would be nice to be in a hurricane
Regardless of whether or not someone has seen a sunspot
As their dead and decomposing body was carried by the current
To the lands of the Climate Deniers and the setting sun
(Which by the way is also due for a lingering fiery death,
Before perhaps becoming a black hole where at least it won't
rain)

Now I've almost made it through (*this sestina*) without any rain
And there is not the slightest hint of a hurricane
So have plastic and pollution condemned us to an early death
While scientists sit and study the source of the sunspot?
(Which any blooming fool knows must be the sun...
Or perhaps my scientific knowledge is not current?)

Does death await us through wind and rain
While current news hits us like a hurricane
And the sunspot moves on the face of the sun?

WRITING EXERCISES

Writing exercises are a fun way to keep your writing tools sharp. There are many different types of exercises available – some are incredibly tricky and require a bit of thought, and some are designed to jump into quickly. Both types are equally useful but some will be more suited to you personally so it's worth trying a few different types to find out which you prefer. To get you started we've included several different exercises to choose from. They've been divided roughly into three types: trigger statements, technical challenges and poetry.

Trigger statements are intended to get you going without having to come up with the start by yourself. You can use the principle to create your own trigger statements once you get the hang of it. Set your own time limit but start low and build up. For these type of exercises ten minutes is a good place to start, but the longer you allow yourself, the more you can produce. As with all of these exercises, sometimes it's just to get you writing, but occasionally your output gives you an idea for something else.

An example of a trigger statement: Use one of the following as a prompt, and write the rest of the story.

- It was then that she realised the truth. She bolted out of the door and drove straight to the...
- Who was coming around the corner? What were they carrying? What will happen when they get there?
- Who was driving the car? Why was it out of control? Who else was in the car?
- Describe your childhood bedroom.
- No rules: Pick a rule/law/norm of society that we take for granted, and write about a world where that rule doesn't exist.
- Take a fictional character from literature and reverse their famous character trait (e.g. Sherlock Holmes

becomes a useless detective, Willy Wonka becomes a diabetic, Dracula faints at the sight of blood).

- Holiday collapse: Write a short story that takes place on your favourite holiday, where nothing goes to plan.
- Firsts: Write about your first time at something. It can be a first kiss, first birthday, first fight, first day of school or work – whatever 'first' interests you most.

Technical challenges are designed to encourage you to fit specific parameters to your output. Where the trigger statements encourage free and mostly unrestrained prose, you will need to ensure you are meeting the parameters of the requirement. Remember, it's supposed to be fun, so try not to make it too difficult for yourself in the beginning.

- Write a eulogy for a sandwich, to be delivered while you are eating it.
- Describe a boring activity in as much detail as possible, trying your hardest not to make it exciting (loading the washing machine, watching paint dry, listening to the grass grow, writing a letter, buying socks).
- Produce a manifesto and some policies for a political party, which would appeal to writers and lovers of the English language.
- Pick a vowel and a consonant, then write for five minutes without using either of those letters.
- List some objects you don't like to touch, then provide some adjectives and verbs for the object, and then create a simile or metaphor to reflect what the object reminded you of.
- Write two independent short pieces. One should contain three lies and one truth, and the other should contain three truths and one lie.
- Making metaphors: Make three columns of lists – one for adjectives (eg: *scrambled, empty, withered, sour, dark*);

one for concrete nouns (eg: *outlet, doghouse, medicine, hook, clock*); one for abstract nouns (eg: *sadness, grief, apology, hope, anxiety*). When you have enough of these lists, you should create a new list, a list of metaphors. Example metaphors: The empty outlet of anxiety. The withered doghouse of grief. The empty medicine of hope. The scrambled medicine of anxiety. And so on.

- Monkey writing (stream of consciousness) is an exercise in letting your creativity do the driving without stopping to correct anything coming out of your fingers. Using a trigger word – for example a song title or any other inspiring idea – just put your pen to paper and let your imagination do the work. The important rules for this are: (a) don't think about what you're writing, (b) do not go back and edit while you're writing it, (c) do not go back and correct spelling/grammar, (d) set yourself an amount of time (start at five minutes and increase it over time) and stop exactly on the timer. Only at this point should you go back and read what you have written. This is not an easy exercise to get going with as it requires you to trust your imagination. However, once you get the hang of it, you'll never look back.

Poetry. As a poet, you could – or should – use some of the previous exercises, but there are also poetry-specific exercises that can be used, some of which are listed below:

- 13 × 13 × 13: Choose the 13th book on your bookshelf, open to page 13, find the 13th sentence, and use it in a poem about luck that is 13 lines long.
- Scrabble Grab: Take 15 random scrabble tiles. Write down a word that begins with each letter. Then write a 15-line poem, including one of your 15 words in each line.
- Musical poem: Find a piece of instrumental music, and listen to it as you write, to inspire your poem.

Allow the breaks or shifts in the music to lead your line breaks and punctuation.

- Take a song you know and write a new verse.
- Senses working overtime – the language of poetry. This exercise will help you to pay attention to the smaller things around you. Make five sensory observations for each sense, as in the examples below:
  - o I see … square white tiles; the backs of strangers; endless rows of books; a lonely microphone; shadows of chairs.
  - o I hear … chattering voices; espresso machines gurgling; dishes clattering, softly, just clinking together; laughter; the crinkle of newspapers.
  - o I feel … brick wall under my arm; a warm cup in my hand; hot air blowing against my face; the hard seat against my bottom; a wooden curve across my back.
  - o I smell … coffee; cinnamon lip balm (smells better than it tastes); used books; vanilla coffee drops; baking bread.
  - o I taste … a mild coffee flavour; a hint of honey; the thickness of hot air; a newly opened book; a tannin tongue.

In our monthly meetings, we always start the session with an exercise, which takes about ten minutes to complete. Once the time is up, we go around the table. Those who wish to may share their writing with the others. Any feedback from the listeners is always friendly and constructive.

AUTHOR BIOGRAPHIES

Helena Abblett

Mark Acton claims that the reason he put his underpants on the outside of his trousers was that he was fighting crime. He is a liar. Don't listen to him. For this and other reasons, I suggest you do not read his work. It's rubbish. It will make you feel unclean.

A former police officer and detective, **Bob Barker** is a founder-member of the Vale Royal Writers Group and its current Chairperson. A crime novelist writing under the name, Robert F Barker, he likes to write gritty crime stories, for which his previous experiences stand him in good stead. In 2015 he published his first novel, *Last Gasp* – the first of an introductory trilogy to his DCI Jamie Carver series. The second book, *Final Breath,* was published in 2017, with the third, *Out Of Air*, being published in early 2018. All are available as either e-books or paperbacks via the Amazon bookstore. Bob lives locally with his family but spends part of each year in Cyprus where he draws inspiration for a series of yet-to-be-published, Cyprus-based thrillers.

Debbie Bennett tells lies and makes things up. Sometimes people pay her for it. Writing fantasy and dark crime/thrillers (as DJ Bennett), Debbie also has an IMDb script-writing credit for a *Dr Who* spin-off DVD. She claims to get her inspiration from the day job – but if she told you about that, she'd have to kill you afterwards … www.debbiebennett.co.uk

Tonia Bevins, sand-grown in Blackpool, has lived in Northwich since 1981. She worked at the BBC and later as an ESOL teacher. She's had a handful of poems published in magazines. She enjoys – and is terrified by – performing at open mic events. She wishes she could play the saxophone and juggle instead. She helps organise VRWG's Wordfests.

David Bruce: Once upon a time I was a chemist, a technologist and technical writer but now I'm a writer and storyteller. Writing and telling my own material in storytelling clubs, at private and public events; for entertainment, as a fund raiser or anywhere there is a sympathetic audience of any age. Continue the ancient craft of oral storytelling with fresh material. They say there are only seven basic plots in the whole world and reading and appreciating the great store of folk tales and myths from around the world often provides my inspiration. An idea from here and an idea from there reworked and remodelled often develop into a totally new adventure whilst keeping to a traditional style.

Steven Capstick has been a member of VRWG for just over two years and took up writing after retirement from teaching. Although he is working on longer pieces that one day will hopefully materialise as a novel, he enjoys writing flash fiction. He hopes that trying to communicate an idea or feeling in as few as words as possible, while challenging, will be a good discipline to develop.

Mac Carding is a Weaver lock keeper who took up writing to fill the time between boats on rainy days. She lives near to Northwich with her husband, is a keen organic gardener and supporter of Greenpeace.

Joan Carter is a prolific reader who hopes one day to write a decent short story. This is her second published attempt.

A founder member of VRWG, **Joan Dowling** has enjoyed many happy years with the group – which is as supportive, stimulating and inspirational as ever. From an abandoned novel, followed by some early success with short story publication, she is now enjoying the challenge of condensing her stories even further and is a big fan of Flash Fiction. Picture Books are also a new and exciting goal on the horizon. For someone who loves words, she seems to be doing her best to avoid them as much as possible!

Les Green is a keen writer, but claims he is better known by his pen name of 'Anon', under which he insists he has written many well-known songs, poems and toilet graffiti. He also claims to have invented swearing while on a drunken week-end in Llandudno, and is quite fond of a nicely browned pie.

Joyce Ireland still lives with the same husband she has had for the past 55 years; born in Lancashire, now living in Cheshire, she mainly studies and writes about the history of North-West England, factually and fictionally. Favourite writing place: Gladstone's Library, Flintshire. Favourite writing tool: fountain pen. Favourite fuel: white wine.

Tom Ireland was born a long time ago. He avoided the coal and salt mines, pretended to be a soldier and a student and a power station labourer and eventually became a teacher because of the high pay, light work load, and long holidays. This gave him time to play badminton, ride a bicycle, and write the *Malinding Village* series of books about life in Sub-Saharan Africa.

Shantele Janes

Liz Leech has lived in Cheshire for the past twenty-six years. Trained in Fine Art & Design, a painter and gilder by profession, she's the writer of the odd poem or short story in between designing the flyers for VRWG's biannual Wordfest events held at the Blue Cap.

Linda Leigh has lived in Northwich all her life, happily married to Geoff since 1974, who is supportive and encouraging in all areas of Linda's dream to publish a novel. Linda grew up by the River Dane in Water Street and used to spend much of her childhood playing on the Oldest Football Ground in the UK, Northwich Victoria which was at the back of Water Street, now sadly new houses have been built on the site . Linda has always been passionate about reading novels and writing creatively whether or on scraps of paper or composing inside her imaginative mind, whilst driving up the M6 to look after her grandaughter Autumn, she finds it totally impossible to precis any pieces of written work or speech for that matter!! Often finds herself the butt of jokes for writing long messages inside cards and when telling a story to family and friends is often asked to get to the point!!! Authors right to spin yarns and make stories up as we tell our tales!! Linda has been retired for 4 years and is busy enjoying life with Geoff and thought naively that she would have heaps of time to write, but an active Springer/Collie dog and the arrival of their first grandchild have completely filled the days and nights, however, Linda is determined to keep on writing and using even more creativity from the fun that retired life brings!!!

Shauna Leishman originally from Northern California (other side of the state from Hollywood and sunny beaches) found herself moving on average every two years throughout her adult life until she finally washed up onto England's Cheshire county seventeen years ago and … stopped moving. It took her at least ten years to realise this. She looks forward to getting up in a morning and filling up a day and always enjoys encounters with English humour and going to Wales.

Gwili Lewis is a bilingual West Walian, a one-time library assistant who in 1949 switched to civic entertainment, serving in Cardiff and Ebbw Vale, before coming to Northwich as manager of the Memorial Hall in 1961. He has written talks and sketches for radio as well as articles for national magazines such as *Evergreen* and *People's Friend*.

Deborah K Mitchell has been writing stories since she was knee high to a flea, and even had a piece published in the Liverpool Echo once. Unfortunately, it was so long ago that she can't remember what it was called, or what it was about. She does remember being given a nice certificate though. Since then, Deborah has carried on writing stories – made up ones, and proper, factual ones; the latter, during her career as a Broadcast Journalist. She has also written four novels – all of which will be self-published on Amazon. At some point.

Carolyn O'Connell

Liz Sandbach is a freelance technical and scientific editor who relishes the opportunity to escape from left-brain thinking by writing creatively. She has been an active member of VRWG for the past thirteen years and also of the North West Poems and Pints scene. She divides her time between Cheshire and the Dordogne. Liz lives in hope that one day Colin Firth will come to his senses and realise his true destiny – but failing that, Dominic Cooper will do!

Marian Smith lives in Warrington and works for an IT company. She has recently completed the first draft of a novel – it only took seven years. She now works part time and is planning on retiring later this year. This will give her more time for writing so, with luck, her next literary effort will only take three years to complete.

David H. Varley is a gentleman scholar and author, or rather would like to be except that it doesn't pay the bills. He is perhaps best known for his masterful translation of *Mastering the Art of French Cooking* into Klingon and for composing an opera based on the life of Marcel Marceau, but otherwise can usually be found writing sci-fi, fantasy and horror. He hopes to finish writing his novel before he expires of old age.

Bill Webster is just over 60 years of age chronologically, albeit not mentally or intellectually, and lives in Cheshire with his wife Helen. He enjoys surfing and shooting, but not at the same time.

Nemma Wollenfang is an MSc Postgraduate and prize-winning short story writer who volunteers at a local animal rescue, Paws Inn, Weaverham – where, incidentally, *Curiosus Cattus* came into being. Her work has appeared in several venues, including three of Flame Tree's bestselling Gothic Fantasy hardbacks: *Science Fiction Short Stories, Murder Mayhem* and *Pirates & Ghosts*. A finalist of several novel awards, she also holds a Silver Honourable Mention from Writers of the Future. She can be found on Facebook, Amazon, Goodreads and Twitter: @NemmaW.

25689466R00112

Printed in Poland
by Amazon Fulfillment
Poland Sp. z o.o., Wrocław